BUG HUNTS
SURVIVING AND COMBATING THE ALIEN MENACE

MARK LATHAM

INTERIOR ILLUSTRATIONS BY ARU-MOR
COVER ILLUSTRATION BY DARREN TAN

First published in Great Britain in 2015 by Osprey Publishing,
PO Box 883, Oxford, OX1 9PL, UK
PO Box 3985, New York, NY 10185-3985, USA
E-mail: info@ospreypublishing.com

Osprey Publishing, part of Bloomsbury Publishing Plc

© 2015 Osprey Publishing Limited

All rights reserved. Apart from any fair dealing for the purpose of private study, research, criticism or review, as permitted under the Copyright, Designs and Patents Act, 1988, no part of this publication may be reproduced, stored in a retrieval system, or transmitted in any form or by any means, electronic, electrical, chemical, mechanical, optical, photocopying, recording or otherwise, without the prior written permission of the copyright owner. Inquiries should be addressed to the Publishers.

The Publisher has made every attempt to secure the appropriate permissions for material reproduced in this book. If there has been any oversight we will be happy to rectify the situation and written submission should be made to the Publishers. All uncredited images are assumed to be in the public domain.

A CIP catalog record for this book is available from the British Library

Print ISBN: 978 1 4728 1071 7
PDF e-book ISBN: 978 1 4728 1072 4
EPUB e-book ISBN: 978 1 4728 1073 1

Typeset in Garamond Pro and Briem Akademi
Originated by PDQ Media, Bungay, UK
Printed in China through Worldprint Ltd.

15 16 17 18 19   10 9 8 7 6 5 4 3 2 1

Osprey Publishing/Shire Publications supports the Woodland Trust, the UK's leading woodland conservation charity. Between 2014 and 2018 our donations will be spent on their Centenary Woods project in the UK.

www.ospreypublishing.com

CONTENTS

Introduction	4
The Alien Menace	7
Draper's World Xeno-Parasites	
Centauran Araknyds	
Hive-Beasts of Klaatu VI	
Bugs of the Galaxy	
Infamous Infestations – A Timeline of Bug Hunts	46
STAR Industries and the Pan-System Marine Corps	51
Remit & Jurisdiction	
Organization & Standard Operating Procedures	
Tactics	
Weapons & Equipment	
Vehicles & Spacecraft	

INTRODUCTION

They said there were no monsters, but there are.

Since first reaching out to the stars, mankind has wondered about the vastness of the galaxy, and asked itself the only question that really mattered: "Are we alone?" In the late 23rd century, after colonizing most of the solar system and visiting worlds even farther afield, we received our answer. But what we were faced with was not an advanced intelligence, nor even primitive beasts to be subjugated to humanity's manifest destiny, but something altogether more terrifying.

Bugs. The term was coined by a private security detail who first encountered a sentient alien species on Draper's World, in the HD 40307 system, in AD 2239. The encounter was brief and violent, and only a handful of the detail escaped with their lives, along with only one of the 13 astro-geologists they were protecting. Half of the survivors died of a mysterious illness before reaching the Kepler Deep Space Research facility, and those that survived underwent further alarming transformations in secure quarantine. As a result, their attackers were identified as a highly aggressive Xeno-Parasite, capable of infecting human biology with previously unknown viral contaminants, and of implanting its eggs into a living human host. Though the word "bugs" stuck as a catch-all term for the weird and varied beasts of the galaxy, it certainly does not convey the full weight of the threat carried by these creatures.

Over the next 50 years, as humans left Earth in greater numbers to form work colonies in distant systems, dozens more bug species were discovered. Of these, only two presented a threat comparable to (or even greater than) the Xeno-Parasites. These were the Centauran Araknyds and the Hive-Beasts of Klaatu – both of which seemed capable of higher thought processes, and, alarmingly, deep space travel. Unlike the Xeno-Parasites, which managed to spread to disparate worlds by means of infected human hosts, the other creatures were able to exist in the cold void of space, and to travel to systems before attacking them in vast swarms. As contact with these species increased, and battles raged, system-wide incursions by these bugs became more frequent, undoubtedly targeting human colonies with malign intelligence.

As soon as the Earth-based government, the Pan-System Authority, reluctantly addressed the possibility of an intelligent extra-terrestrial threat, they set about finding a way to meet it. Interstellar defense was an area with

(OPPOSITE)
STAR marine in full kit sweeping a research facility during the Io incident.

COLONIZING THE GALAXY

The first sub-light drives capable of sending manned flights beyond the solar system were developed by Stellar Dynamic, culminating in twin launches in 2116. The journeys were long and arduous, and after several "generation ships" managed to establish successful research colonies in the Tau Ceti system, mankind finally had a jumping-off point for further expansion and exploration. Advances in cryo-sleep technology eventually did away with generation ships, allowing crew members to remain frozen in hypersleep for journeys of up to 30 years, with their huge research ships guided by advanced navicom AI. However, even this was not ideal, as crews would become estranged from their families and homeworld, and often displayed severe psychological issues as a result of prolonged space sickness.

Finally, in 2210, the waning Stellar Dynamic merged with the emergent Ark Industries, and set about developing the first interstellar drive, based on theoretical designs that had remained unrealized for over two centuries. A chance discovery led to the unlocking of this fringe technology, and the newly formed mega-corporation, STAR Industries, held the key to human expansion throughout the galaxy. Distant colonies were reinforced, and brought back into the terrestrial fold by means of a hyperlane network; formerly off-limits worlds were mined for natural resources by massive industrial operations; deep space research stations and spacecraft docking hubs were built throughout the interstellar "highways." Mankind seemed set for limitless dominion over the galaxy. That is, until the first bugs were encountered. Overnight, humanity went from rulers of an endless territory to terrified children sheltering in the dark from an unknowable, alien evil...

little investment up to that point, and franchised colonial defense forces – often rag-tag bands of mercenaries or retired soldiers – were all that stood between the outer colonies and the ravening hordes of bugs scratching at the door. With this as an incentive, the major galactic mega-corporations made bids to privatize humanity's galactic military presence. After two years of negotiations, during which time more fringe colonies were snuffed out like candle lights in the darkness, STAR Industries won the contract, and an elite fighting force of pan-system marines was assembled, ready to take the threat to the enemy.

Whatever the mission, whatever the odds, the STAR marines stand ready to face the threat – and bug-hunting is their specialty.

THE ALIEN MENACE

The greatest problem we face in planning the fight against bugs, is that the bugs do not read their manuals, nor do they feel any obligation to follow doctrine. Thankfully, there's no problem that cannot be solved by the use of high explosives.
– Colonel Abraham T. Stokeley, 5th Arcturian Regiment, STAR Pan-System Marine Corps

Bugs have been encountered across the galaxy, in many forms and many environments. Though each species has unique traits, abilities, and physical characteristics that mark them from other bug races, they all hold one thing in common, namely that they are utterly relentless, aggressive, and voracious predators. They cannot be reasoned with; their minds, such that they are, are so unutterably alien that their motives cannot be discerned, and their tactics – if indeed they employ them – are almost impossible to predict.

The Pan-System Authority, the central administration of the human galactic government, has ordered that all strains of these "intelligent" bugs be wiped from the galaxy, in order for mankind to realize its manifest destiny. And yet the bugs don't make it easy – it is their very nature to infest whatever world they come into contact with. Wherever a space station, derelict vessel, or lunar colony is cleansed of a bug presence, two more nests appear nearby. For every bug killed, there are a million more to take its place. For this reason, the STAR marines have earned the moniker of "the Exterminators," for their role has become increasingly specialized over the decades of the 23rd century, so that they are now little more than interplanetary pest control.

To date, three main types of sentient bug have been discovered, each seemingly worse than the last, with dozens of lesser species appearing on isolated worlds across colonized space. The first type to be found was the genus known as the Draper's World Xeno-Parasite. This group is particularly feared for its ability to spread across the galaxy in host bodies, using humans as living eggs. In their early contact with humans, they managed to infiltrate several far-flung colonies by implanting their spoor into unsuspecting colonists, who had no idea how to treat the condition, and continued en route to their destination.

The second genus of bug to be found was the Araknyds of the Centaurus Arm. So called because every strain has eight limbs, they are about as far removed from Earth spiders as it is possible to get. Possessed of a keen intellect, some of the bugs appear to be endowed with an extra-sensory psychic power, which they have used to communicate with humans, after a fashion. These bugs appear to be able to travel through space of their own volition, surviving in the hard vacuum indefinitely – a gift they have used to make their way slowly towards Earth, which they perceive as both the greatest threat to their existence, and a source of near-endless food.

Finally, the bizarre Hive-Beasts of Klaatu VI were discovered by an exploratory fleet in the Outer Arm, investigating a large system in the Klaatu Nebula. These crustaceous bugs inhabit several planets, which are covered in gigantic, conical geological formations – somewhat like termite mounds. The creatures are part of what appears to be a hive mind, and are controlled by a sub-species of huge, tunneling creatures. A by-product of their infestations is that their worlds are left mineral-rich, as precious ores essential to human industry are discarded as waste by the creatures. Unfortunately, the Hive-Beasts are not only highly intelligent, but utterly devoted to protecting their territory from intruders.

Draper's World Xeno-Parasites

The discovery of the Xeno-Parasites on Draper's World represented a paradigm shift in the way human explorers viewed alien life. Up until that point, the only extra-terrestrial life encountered by mankind had been primordial micro-bacteria, and simple, single-celled organisms. Now, the very real threat of a dangerous, tough, and ultra-hostile alien menace had to be recognized.

The astro-geological research team, led by Dr. Franz O'Keefe, had touched down on HD 40307b during the planet's autumnal equinox. At that time, volcanic activity on the world was at its lowest ebb for the annual cycle, and Dr. O'Keefe theorized that a temporary base camp could be set up on the surface for at least a three-month expedition, before seismic and volcanic eruptions would threaten the operation. The mission comprised 13 scientists, and a lightly armed six-man security detail, there to ensure the safety of the scientists from natural disasters as much as potential alien life. The assignment of private security forces had been a standard requirement since the discovery of the first simple organisms, as the potential for encountering hostile life-forms was recognized, even if no-one truly believed the reality of it.

The first six Earth-weeks passed without incident. Though the planet was somewhat more volatile than expected, the base camp was located in a relatively stable position, sheltered by natural granite rock spires, and the scientists enjoyed a fruitful mission. Draper's World was quickly identified as a source of vital elemental resources rarely found in our own solar system – the abundance of which was so startling that Dr. O'Keefe gave the order to press on further into the planet's hazardous environs to see what else could be found.

(OPPOSITE)
A Xeno-Parasite Soldier in advanced stages of its life-cycle. Note the slashing talons, elongated teeth and bladed tail, all capable of tearing through STAR marine body armour.

Some 30 miles from base camp, a team of four scientists – including O'Keefe – and three guards discovered a labyrinthine cave network at the base of a dormant volcano. The tunnel system (later dubbed "Franz's Folly") stretched for an indefinite distance beneath the planet's surface, and once it was determined that there was no active volcanic threat within, O'Keefe gave the order to explore it, for at least a short distance. After several hours of laborious journeying in the dark, carrying heavy equipment in blistering heat, the team found an underground repository of calcium deposits, and, against all odds, moisture. Buoyed by the fact that the planet might contain underground streams, the team pressed on deeper and deeper, until finally their path terminated at a large cavern filled with a lake of some strange, oleaginous liquid. The pool was black, and potentially many yards deep at its center, and, with nowhere else to go, the scientists set about taking samples instead; and that was when they were attacked.

No-one had seen the shadows moving between the stalagmites on the far side of the lake, nor the faint ripples in the strange primordial ooze, coming closer towards the preoccupied scientists. Dr. Antonia Burren, who had waded knee-deep into the black pool, was suddenly pulled beneath the surface by a force unseen. When the security detail tried to extract her, only her torso surfaced, her lower half remaining somewhere beneath the liquid. The first extra-terrestrial erupted from the ooze, and was at first driven back by the guards' gunfire, though the light pistols did little actual damage to it.

Even as the team attempted to pull back, more of the aliens appeared, moving stealthily around the edges of the cavern, and swimming across the lake of ooze. They were squat creatures, perhaps no taller than 5 feet, and with an ape-like gait. That was where the similarities to Earth mammals ended, however, as their limbs were segmented like that of an insect, tipped with long claws; their skin was hard and pitted, and matt black to the point of absorbing all light around them. Their bodies were topped with long, serpentine necks, which tapered to a pointed, eyeless head, and they were possessed of segmented tails, which terminated at a spiked, mace-like appendage. At first, they seemed vaguely humanoid, but as they drew nearer, their victims observed that the creatures had spindly, secondary appendages which curled up to their bony chests – atrophied limbs that were used to grapple their prey close while their long, insectoid arms made short work of other opposition.

As the scientists struggled to disentangle themselves from their

Xeno-Parasites often ensnare live victims close to their nests as a food source to facilitate rapid growth of their Soldiers.

DRAPER'S WORLD

Originally known simply as "Planet B," Draper's World is a mineral-rich, volcanic planet, the second in a small system orbiting the star HD 40307. Located some 42 light years from Earth in the Pictor constellation, the system was singled out as an untapped font of resources. "Planet G" in the same system had already been identified as a so-called super-Earth, and the Kepler Deep Space Research Station was constructed in its orbit to monitor the planet in preparation for terraforming. A small team of astro-geologists, stopping briefly at the Kepler facility, touched down on Draper's World in 2239. Their initial research was fruitful – they discovered an abundance of several otherwise scarce metallurgic elements including coronium, orichalcum, and calculon, making the world rife for plunder. Unfortunately, celebrations were short lived. The astro-geologists were attacked by a parasitic alien beast – the first truly sentient extra-terrestrial to be encountered in almost 150 years of exploration. Thanks to their security detail, one of the scientists made it back to the Kepler facility – but that was only the start of the nightmare! Subsequent attempts to reclaim Draper's World have so far failed.

equipment, the creatures pounced upon them, dragging them beneath the surface of the lake in short order, while others fought a running battle with the security detail as they tried to escort Dr. O'Keefe back through the maze of tunnels. The further the aliens got from their cavern, the less ferocious their attacks became, until the pursuit seemed to drop off altogether. Reaching the cave mouth by which they had entered the tunnels, the two remaining guards and one scientist paused for a moment to catch their breaths, and in that moment a creature struck. It dropped on them from the cliffs above, unperturbed by the baking heat and glaring sunlight of the surface world. Batting aside the security guards, it pinned O'Keefe to the floor, and its head opened up like the petals of some blasphemous flower, revealing rows of tiny sharp teeth within. With no warning, a jagged proboscis shot from the beast's mouth, shattering O'Keefe's visor with ease, and forcing its way down his throat. The guards returned and redoubled their efforts, eventually driving the creature back into the tunnels. Dragging O'Keefe into their surface rover, with its sealed environment, they managed to transport him back to base camp, where he was attended to by the other scientists. Given their limited medical expertise, however, the decision was made to pack up the base camp and return to the Kepler research station, in orbit around HD 40307b.

O'Keefe was placed, comatose, into a quarantined medical bay on the planetary light-lander *Socrates,* while the remainder of the team broke down the camp. However, as the orange sun sank below the horizon and night fell, the astro-geologists realized they were not alone. In less than an hour, the aliens had overrun the camp and killed – or captured – every man and woman bar two; two security guards, realizing all hope was lost for the scientists, fought their way to the *Socrates* and blasted off, leaving behind Draper's World and its hideous native fauna forever – or so they thought.

The Kepler Incident

The Kepler Deep Space Research Station (DSRS) is one of the largest and best equipped off-world scientific facilities in the Pictor sub-sector. Staffed by over 100 micro-biologists, geologists, astro-physicists, and their support staff, the facility provides a launchpad for all scientific voyages in the stellar region.

Once at the station, Dr. O'Keefe's condition was quickly stabilized in the facility's quarantine bay. Held on life support for a full day, he soon showed signs of recovery, and came out of his coma remarkably quickly. His physical wounds were minimal, although his synaptic responses were sluggish, and he struggled to adjust to his surroundings. On the second day, a nurse in full hazmat gear was sent to take a sample of O'Keefe's blood. As she did so, O'Keefe's body began to blotch and blister, as though his blood was boiling. As the nurse tried to calm O'Keefe and call for assistance, the geologist vomited a torrent of boiling-hot blood over her, which burned her even through the protective suit. The blood contained thousands of tiny, spider-like creatures, which scuttled through the medi-bay in droves, swarming around the doors and reinforced windows, and eating through the hermetic seals as if they were nothing. In minutes, the swarm of bugs was scurrying through the facility – through air ducts, corridors, and maintenance shafts. And while the crew frantically tried to kill or capture them, no-one saw what was happening in the medi-bay.

O'Keefe, somehow still alive, had taken leave of his senses, and was grappling with the already traumatized nurse. In a shower of gore, O'Keefe's stomach exploded, and three vicious little creatures leapt from his body and instantly began tearing apart the unfortunate nurse, rapidly gorging themselves on her flesh like a shoal of piranhas, before scurrying away to find a hiding place. These creatures were more aggressive and far stronger than the parasites encountered so far, and were characterized by enlarged teeth and claws, earning them the moniker of 'Soldiers'.

The battle to keep control of the facility raged for days. The resourceful scientists and their security staff hunted down as many of the miniscule spiders as they could, and sent out distress calls to any nearby Authority vessels that were listening. But as the days passed, the spider-like creatures underwent rapid changes. Security sweeps began to find larger creatures, bearing the distinctive characteristics of the aliens back on Draper's World. These creatures shunned conflict and fled to the bowels of the station. When the security staff found their lair, they found that dozens of science personnel, missing or feared dead, had been cocooned in a sticky, calcium-rich ooze, suspended from the ceiling of the lower stores, where they served as a food supply for the aliens – a living food supply. The guards had had little time to process this information when they were attacked by a seemingly new form of alien life – three tall, gangrel creatures, all teeth, claws, and lashing tails. Later identified as adult Soldiers, having undergown rapid development, these beasts seemed hell-bent on protecting the smaller creatures, and those guards who survived the

(OPPOSITE)
Mature Xeno-Parasite Drone, with its mouth-section opened to reveal leech-like teeth and an egg-laying proboscis.

encounter could only retreat to the station's secure command center, where they waited with the terrified scientists for help to arrive

The Seeds Are Sown

It took almost five weeks to bring the Kepler facility back under Authority control, as all they could do was bolster the security forces on board whilst

THE XENO-PARASITE LIFE-CYCLE

The parasites (*Xeno Parasitus Volcanis*) are an incredibly hardy species, and it is easy to see how they spread insidiously throughout Authority territory before their true nature was discerned.

Drones are the most long-lived of the Xeno-Parasite sub-species. By means of hibernating in a sealed, calcium-rich cocoon, it is surmised that a Drone can survive dormant for many centuries with no food source, in the most extreme environmental conditions. Despite having no visual or olfactory organs, they are incredibly sensitive to vibrations and minute temperature change, and can sense when prey is nearby. This brings a dormant Drone to life, and it will systematically hunt its prey. Its immediate purpose is to gather a food supply for its nest and offspring; its secondary objective is to implant one or more of its victims with eggs, by means of its vicious spike-like proboscis. Victims that are implanted fall into a deep coma, usually lasting for around 24 Earth-hours. When they awake, their blood – now tainted with the Xeno-Parasite's own DNA – begins to increase in temperature. Once it reaches boiling point, a chain reaction is set into motion. First, the victim vomits a swarm of infant Drones in a torrent of his own boiling blood. These set about finding a place to hide, or easy victims to feed upon, until they have grown in strength.

Next, still alive, the victim involuntarily staggers towards the nearest source of food for his parasitic masters. Once he is in close proximity, the three eggs within him grow with extreme rapidity, and the newborn Soldiers burst out of his stomach, killing the host instantly. The Soldiers gorge on their victims, and possess incredible strength given their small size. Through a process of "shedding," the Soldiers grow to ten times their embryonic size within 24–72 hours, depending on how much food is available, at which point they begin to capture living hosts for the Drones to feed on.

Where the chance of establishing a successful colony seems low, the tiny, infant Drones are capable of implanting a handful of eggs into a host by means of a small, yet painful, bite. Undetectable for weeks, these microscopic eggs actively evade detection in the host's bloodstream, moving like nanites. In this way, the Xeno-Parasites were able to infect over a dozen Kepler DSRS scientists without their knowing – later, these scientists traveled to other facilities or colonies, where the parasites finally hatched. Without Soldiers to protect them, the chances of success are slim, but thanks to mankind's advances in space travel, the Xeno-Parasites have been able to gain a foothold on worlds far beyond their point of origin.

At least one in every 300 infant Drones develops into a Queen. This is the weakest of the three strains, although they will always fight each other to the death until only one remains. Queens are capable of bio-forming the locale into a more conducive environment, vomiting forth pools of gestation fluid, and creating massive egg-sacs to which they attach themselves, before laying countless Drone eggs. In the absence of a Queen, the Drones will hibernate until they are able to start the process again. With a Queen present, however, the entire species shows signs of higher intellectual function; they become able to direct their efforts efficiently and effectively even against an organized military force.

waiting for a detachment of Earth's army to arrive. During that time, the bugs multiplied, using the captured scientists as living hosts. The more numerous strain – called 'Drones' – grew in number, and at least one was observed to have rapidly evolved into a 'Queen', much like an Earth-native ant. This Queen gave birth to other Drones, and even began to transform the fabric of the station to an environment more conducive to Xeno-Parasite life. None of the combat personnel were trained for the task at hand, and the early skirmishes went badly for the humans as the military underestimated the bugs' resilience. Finally, they resorted to a scorched earth policy, rendering parts of the facility utterly useless by detonating smart grenades and venting entire hull sections into space.

Once victory was secured, and the Pan-System Authority reviewed the incident, the Kepler facility underwent a massive refit, taking almost a year. During this time, the survivors, after debriefing, were sent to work in research colonies in other parts of the sub-sector and beyond. What no-one could have guessed – and even the best medical technology couldn't detect – was that the Xeno-Parasites were capable of implanting a secondary infection within suitable hosts, which lay dormant for days, weeks, or even months before emerging. Even before the Authority's security review was complete, distress calls began to flood in from ten far-flung worlds, separated by hundreds of light years. The Xeno-Parasites had spread, and over the coming decades would continue to do so. Mankind's own innovations in interstellar travel had given the aliens the perfect platform to infest the galaxy.

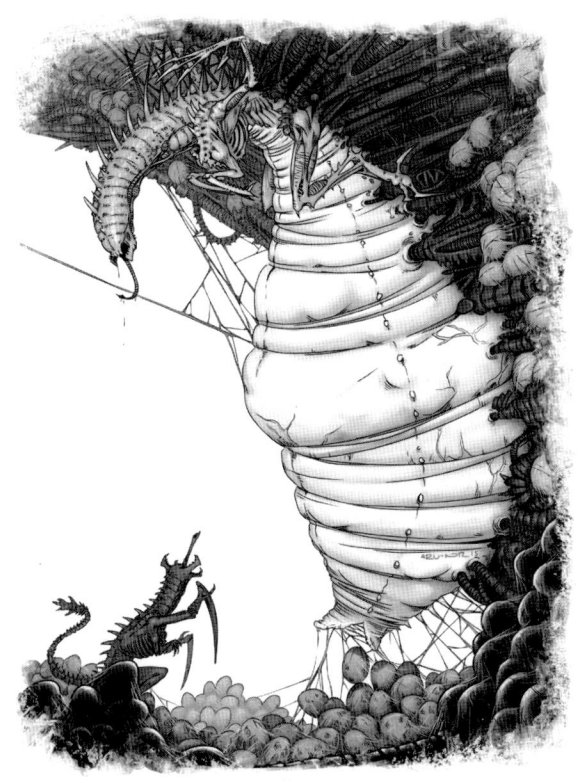

A Xeno-Parasite Queen attached to its egg-sac.

Combating the Threat

After the Kepler Incident, several small Xeno-Parasite incursions were reported across the galaxy. It was four years before the first STAR marines were deployed in a bug-infested warzone, and when they were, the lessons learned from their somewhat inadequate predecessors were immediately put into practice. The Xeno-Parasites, however, taught the STAR Marine Corps that standardized "bug-hunting" tactics were virtually useless, and that every species of bug required the use of specialist tactics and the deployment of tailored hardware load-outs to effectively eradicate them.

All of the strains of Xeno-Parasite have a high level of resistance to energy and flame-based weaponry, largely due to the bugs' tough exo-skeletons and the unique composition of the alien blood. Xeno-Parasite blood (if it can be called such) is more akin to lava, being a highly toxic and thixotropic mix of molten metal, enriched with calcium and sulfur. Their internal body temperature runs between 1112 and 1652°F (600 and 940°C), making them immune to the effects of extreme temperatures and most hostile environments. Cooling their outer shells with concentrated blasts of nitrogen can make the creatures sluggish, though it cannot incapacitate them fully. One of the more peculiar traits of the species has been discovered within the Soldier strain. These creatures have virtually no external pain receptors, as evinced by several documented exchanges with STAR marines in which the bugs had limbs blown off and continued to fight. However, internally it is a different story. Uniquely amongst their species, the Soldiers seem to feel the pain of their own magma-like blood, living with extreme internal burning for their entire sorry existence. This curse of evolution, Earth's exo-biologists postulate, drives Xeno-Parasite Soldiers into a near-permanent state of rage of madness – if, of course, they are capable of such emotion.

STAR marines understand that Xeno-Parasites are not to be engaged in close combat except in the most desperate circumstances. Although Drones and Queens are not much stronger than a man, the Soldiers certainly are, and the boiling blood of all three strains is a very real combat hazard, capable of reducing even polymer blades to molten slag in moments. As a result of battles against Xeno-Parasites, marines are often kitted out with Kevlar-weave heat-resistant fatigues along with their usual body armor, although its efficacy is dubious.

Xeno-Parasites tend to gather in confined spaces, and therefore opportunities to bring heavy weapons to bear are limited (the attack on Perdition Alpha being a notable exception). With time to prepare, the most effective combat measures to employ against the Draper's World bugs are sentry guns and heavy exo-suit troopers.

Despite the undoubted efficiency of the STAR marines' military response, the Xeno-Parasites always seem to find a way to survive. Sometimes they will re-emerge upon a world long thought cleared of all alien nests. Other times an infection will occur on a previously unaffected colony, or on a bulk spacecraft light years from home. The Xeno-Parasite is like the mythical Hydra – you can cut off one head, but two more grow to take its place. Thanks to mankind, this aggressive and tenacious species now has a secure foothold in many parts of the galaxy.

Centauran Araknyds

The RSGC2 cluster of red giant stars, also known as Stephenson's Reach, is something of a galactic anomaly located within the Centaurus galactic arm. It had long been coveted by STAR Industries, as its hundreds of planets, planetoids, and super-sized meteorites were believed to hold not just a wealth of alien mineral deposits, but also myriad simple life-forms that would prove invaluable to mankind's advances into bio-technology. The majority of those worlds were so hostile to human life, and so eternally bathed in the dull red

(OPPOSITE)
Captain Ana Carter of Zero Platoon, surveying the infested facility at Perdition Alpha.

glow of the giant stars, that the region became known as Hell's Reach by the long-haul exploration parties and ill-fated terraformers sent to study it. Six separate expeditions were sent to Hell's Reach over a 15-year period, and every one was forced to abandon its mission owing to unforeseen circumstances. When the fourth mission vanished without a trace while attempting to establish a research base on the remote planetoid of Lycea, the region earned

ATTACK ON PERDITION ALPHA

The Perdition system, approximately 2.6 parsecs rimward of Barnard's Star, seems an unusually isolated and backwater world for a major STAR Marine Corps engagement. However, upon a remote fracking colony on this far-flung ice world, the marines completed their greatest ever victory against the Xeno-Parasites, at great cost.

After three unsuccessful attempts to eradicate Xeno-Parasite infestations from human colonies, STAR Marine Command had come up with a variety of possible new tactics. When a distress call was picked up from Perdition's Alpha Station in early 2248, the chance to put those tactics into use was seized.

A platoon of marines under the corps' poster-child, Captain Ana Carter, made planetfall two klicks from Perdition Alpha, setting up a mobile firebase before sending two fireteams into the station. There, the marines discovered 60 survivors of the station's 205-man complement barricaded in the central comms tower, and a network of cramped corridors and mining tunnels swarming with bug Soldiers.

The sub-levels of Ice Station Alpha had been transformed by the Xeno-Parasites. Whole sections of the basements were flooded with viscous ooze, much like the underground lake found on Draper's World. The aliens had huddled close to the facility's power core, seeking out warmth and creating a nest for themselves. Walls and ceilings were covered in calcium-rich deposits, which seemed to act as atmospheric filters. As a result, the air had become poisonous to humans, with most of the oxygen and carbon dioxide from the artificial atmos-processor being replaced with gaseous sulfur. Although the Xeno-Parasites are capable of existing in almost any atmosphere, they had apparently gone to great lengths to make the station more amenable.

The fireteams were unable to gain a foothold in the station itself, and the Xeno-Parasites' attacks prevented them from evacuating the refugees. And so the ultimate sanction was called for – the sacrifice of the human colonists. The order was not issued lightly; STAR Command demanded that the planet – rich in mineral resources and ripe for terraforming – be completely scoured of the alien threat. Marine Corps intelligence suggested that the only way to achieve this goal was to cut the bugs off from any sustainable source of food or hosts, and engage them in open war. The mines and the surrounding facility represented the only viable sources of cover on the entire planet, and if that cover was eliminated, the bugs would have nowhere to hide.

With this in mind, the marines pulled back to their firebase, and detonated three remote smart-nukes in the mines. Although some bugs survived the initial destruction, the marines soon pressed home their advantage, using motorized breacher units and exo-suits to pick through the debris. Uncovering the last remaining Queen and her nest of Soldier bugs, the marines drove the creatures out onto the ice-fields, where they were mown down by heavy weapon teams. The engagement wiped out every Xeno-Parasite on Perdition, at a cost of 60 colonists' lives, an acceptable 12 percent marine casualty rate, and the destruction of a single fracking facility.

a fell reputation, with many fleet captains proclaiming it "cursed," like the fabled Bermuda Triangle of Earth.

STAR Industries, however, were nothing if not persistent. Convinced that untold wealth lay in Hell's Reach, they prepared one of the largest expeditions ever assembled, and dispatched it to RSGC2 in 2246, less than a year after the failure of the previous mission. This time, two large research vessels carrying almost 200 scientists, terraformers, and engineers were dispatched to settle twin colonies on Lycea and its sister object, Pallas. These two tiny, ice-bound planetoids spun in a synchronistic orbit, and STAR Industries hoped not only that the initial survey of those worlds would prove lucrative, but also that later they would make prime fleet bases for further expeditions into the region.

Far from home, on an icy rock where the blizzards never ceased and the snow reflected the blood-red suns, the colonists who set down the first structures on Lycea didn't need to be reminded of the region's devilish nickname.

STAR Industries had secretly been worried about the reasons behind the loss of the fourth Hell's Reach mission, largely due to the strange but indistinct transmissions they had received shortly before losing contact with the expedition. For this reason, the fifth mission was escorted by a single marine platoon of the 12th Lunar Regiment, aboard the Lincoln-class corvette MSS *Bodega*. The marines' mission was highly classified, and the civilian and tech staff – kept in the dark about the reason for the marines' presence – became duly concerned about the nature of their mission. The STAR marines were still an experimental taskforce, though their ranks had swelled with new recruits since the previous year's incursion on the moon Io, too close to home for most people's comfort.

With their ships in orbit around Lycea, the engineering teams were first to the planet, and began laying the foundations for a semi-permanent research station. It was during this initial period of construction – scheduled to last eight days – that a violent meteor storm hit the northern hemisphere of the planetoid. The storm was not predicted by any met-cog scanners, and its sudden appearance cut off all comms with the engineering team for several hours. When the storm subsided and the comms-net was finally brought back online, there was no sign of the engineers. As a precaution, the STAR marines prohibited any civilian search and rescue operation until they had assessed the danger, and two full fireteams made planetfall at the engineers' base camp. Even though they had been warned by HQ of a possible extra-terrestrial threat in the area, they soon discovered that they were woefully underprepared for what came next.

Escape from Lycea

Against the relentless storm of blood-red snow and hail that battered the marines, it was almost impossible to find any trace of life on the surface of Lycea. Their multi-trackers were useless, and the visual targeting matrices

An Araknyd Warrior. Forelimbs are always fused to the bug's organic weaponry. This one is armed with a scythe talon and a 'stinger' – a pistol-like bio-weapon that seems to exhibit low-level intelligence of its own.

in their environmental suits suffered massive interference. In such extreme conditions, the marines had to rely on only their own senses; which is how the bugs got so close before being detected.

Fewer than half the marines present had seen action against bugs before, and certainly never anything like this. From the raging blizzard came a horde of scurrying, clawed creatures, covered in thick bony plates and carrying what looked like weapons – albeit ones made of organic matter. The eight-limbed

Araknyd stingers appear to be living, parasitic organisms. Due to the development of the stinger's brain stem, it is unclear whether the Warriors use these bio-weapons as guns, or whether the guns themselves are the intelligence, guiding their hosts around the battlefield.

bugs looked at first glance like spiders, although the creatures' scaly hide and intricate patternation placed them more akin to large reptiles than arachnids.

Regardless of the aliens' origins, the marines had been trained to do but one thing – squash bugs. With that in mind, despite the odds, they opened fire with everything they had. Lycea, so long a frozen, desolate world, suddenly felt the heat of battle. Flamethrowers scorched the bugs, and carbines tore swathes through their endless, scuttling ranks. For a moment, it looked as though the few marines who had landed would be enough to turn back the swarm; but only for a moment. In the next instant, a flock of winged bugs swept from the snowstorm, hacking at the marines with scythe-like talons and battering into them with their full weight. Sergeant Idaho, a veteran of the Io infestation, authorized the use of the marines' experimental grav-packs, taking to the air with four of his men and deploying their suits' countermeasures to draw the winged creatures away from his team's heavy weapon specialists.

With Idaho drawing heat from the main force, the remaining marines began a fighting retreat to their dropship. However, the warrior-bugs were relentless, seemingly growing in number until they were like a huge writhing shadow looming from the snowstorm. As soon as they drew to close range, the strange weapons opened fire with a barking, screeching sound. Globules of glowing plasma energy lit the air like tracer fire. The organic ammunition, whilst insufficient to punch through the marines' armor, did begin to melt it. Where the glowing ooze struck soft joins in the environment suits, it burned through in moments, opening the marines' suits to the freezing, oxygen-free air. A few were dragged bodily into the dropship, their respirators keeping them alive. Others froze to death mid-battle, their sudden deaths a blessing in disguise as the monsters swarmed over their bodies, hacking and tearing them apart in seconds.

Elsewhere, Sergeant Idaho and his small team successfully shook off the winged bugs and found themselves a defensible position to fight from while their grav-packs charged up for another burst. Unfortunately for them, time was one thing they did not have. Idaho's comms-link crackled to life – the marines who had made it back to the dropship were under attack from something big, and they were prepping for launch to avoid having the crate destroyed by bug firepower. Realizing that he had allowed himself to be drawn too far from the dropship, Idaho ordered his team to pull back as soon as the grav-packs had charged. That's when the ground began to tremble, and one of the big bugs that his men had mentioned came for him.

The creature towered over them, six enormous legs holding up a muscular body; two powerful arms ending in scythe-like claws beginning to smash apart the glacial cover the marines had been sheltering behind. The monster's head was protected by a broad bony crest, giving it the appearance of a hammerhead shark. Bundles of fleshy tubes drooped from its gaping maw, leading to a massive funnel-like protrusion in the beast's chest. And that protrusion began to glow and spark as a super-charged ball of plasma built up inside it, ready to be discharged at the marines.

The grav-packs lit green just as the bug prepared to fire its plasma weapon at the team. Barking an order to the others, Idaho hit his pack and boosted high into the air, as a massive surge of energy ploughed into the glacier behind him. One of his men was burned alive by the glowing green energy, and then Idaho felt the pain surge through his body as he realized he'd been hit. The spray from the monster's chest-weapon had hit him on the leg, burning it off below the knee and knocking out his grav-pack's stabilizers. He corkscrewed to the ground, hitting the ice as the monster bore down on him, claws slashing. The remaining two marines boosted clear, looking back in time to see Sergeant Idaho unloading his carbine into the monster, even as a swarm of smaller bugs swept into the narrow defile. That was the last anyone saw of the Hero of Lycea.

Deadly Pursuit

The dropship jetted from the planetoid's surface, battling the howling storm and coming under intense fire from the sea of bugs below. Plasma weaponry melted holes in the ship's wings, almost bringing them down; but the pilot skillfully brought his crate under control and initiated the thrusters to send them clear of the alien weaponry's effective range. As the storm cleared and the dropship entered Lycea's upper atmosphere, blips began to appear on the ship's scanners. Above them, thousands of orb-like, luminescent creatures floated gracefully, trailing tendrils 100 feet long towards the thin clouds below. There was no time to take evasive action. As the tendrils contacted the ship's hull, the jellyfish-like creatures latched on, pulling themselves in towards the fuselage even as the ship rocketed outwards towards space, collecting dozens of the creatures as it went.

By the time the dropship appeared on the MSS *Bodega's* viewscreens, the horrified marines could only watch as the drifting spores detonated, reducing the dropship to mangled debris, their comrades aboard it killed in an instant.

The remaining marines set their vessel on high alert, and led an emergency council which also included the captain of the research vessel DSS *Belladonna*, and the lead scientist of the expedition, Dr. Albertus Kafka. Even as they discussed pulling out of Lycea's orbit and regrouping with the second engineering team at Pallas, the *Bodega* suffered an impact from an extra-terrestrial object, causing massive damage to the Faster-Than Light (FTL) drive. Helm reported incoming meteorites, slingshotting around Lycea as though they were intentionally being guided towards the cruiser. When a distress signal came in from the crew of the DSS *Augustus* in orbit around Pallas, the marines knew they were facing no ordinary bugs.

In the ensuing chaos, the remaining marines used their cruiser's weaponry to deflect the trajectory of the incoming meteorites while they evacuated to the *Belladonna*. Commandeering the research vessel, they steered away from Lycea's orbit as the *Bodega* was destroyed in their wake and dozens more meteorites flew towards them. Refusing the pleas of the civilian crew to mount a rescue of the stricken DSS *Augustus,* the marines entered hyperspace as soon as they were able, leaving Lycea in the hands of the bugs.

Araknyd Warrior strains utilise a strange type of bio-energy weapon, labelled a 'stinger', which draws power from the creature's own body via a series of organic tubes.

A Relentless Foe

Using vid-captures and comms recordings from the battle on Lycea, STAR Command was able to piece together some information about the eight-legged bugs that Sergeant Idaho's team had fought. When training videos began to circulate around marine bases, the new bugs quickly became known as Araknyds, due to their spider-like appearance, or officially *Xeno Aranea Onocentaurus*. The Marine Corps science and tech division theorized that the creatures did not originate on either Lycea or Pallas, but probably migrated there in the form of spores, locked in frozen meteorites that cycled through Hell's Reach. These meteorites would have been trapped by the gravitational pulls of the many red super-giants in the region, and only by chance would they impact the occasional planet or moon. Perhaps, it was said, the aliens needed some form of atmosphere to develop from tiny spore to fully functioning monster, and the conditions on Lycea – while not ideal – were good enough to allow for the bugs' rapid growth. On airless moons and volcanic worlds, the alien spore would likely be trapped in a form of undeveloped stasis indefinitely.

The idea that the icy meteorites were somehow controlled by the Araknyds was laughed off. The creatures documented on Lycea displayed no means of achieving

such a feat, after all, and the apparent intelligent redirection of the meteorites against the *Bodega*, *Augustus*, and *Belladonna* was put down to a freak meteor shower, the presence of which must have been disguised by radiation from solar flares. However, STAR Command declared Hell's Reach a quarantine zone – even if the bugs couldn't pilot meteorites like spaceships, they were still likely to be infesting any number of planets, moons, and asteroids in the region. The numbers observed on Lycea alone made open military action in the sector a practical impossibility. Better to leave Hell's Reach and its denizens alone, at least for the time being.

Twenty years passed before the Araknyds were encountered again, but it was not in Hell's Reach. Further coreward, in the Wild Duck Cluster of the Scutum Reaches, a STAR marine patrol of the fringe colonies received a distress signal from a herculanium mining colony on the planet Barnard-E32. When the marines arrived at the planet, they found it surrounded by the giant, floating spores that had previously been described in the outer atmosphere of Lycea. An unmanned probe to the planet's surface confirmed the worst – the factory complex, stretching over 5 cubic miles, was infested with Araknyds. Before the probe was destroyed, it had scanned more than 100,000 alien lifeforms within the complex. Within hours, huge ice-meteorites began to encircle the planet, slingshotting around the orbit of Barnard-E32 and into the path of the marine patrol. A light-squeezed transmission from STAR Command sanctioned the use of a nuclear bombardment of the planet, and ordered that all potentially infected meteorites be destroyed. A vital work colony, 50 years in the making, was wiped out virtually overnight, because the risk of the Araknyds spreading to other worlds in the system was too terrible to think about. When more – and larger – meteorites were detected heading into the system from beyond the sub-sector, a semi-permanent taskforce was assigned to patrol the valuable assets of the Wild Duck Cluster, and STAR Industries sub-contracted the building of Sobieski's Shield – the most widespread early-warning defense grid ever built outside the Sol system, covering a vast area containing nine systems.

The Norma-36 system contains one of the oldest outer colonies, having been established during the very first wave of interstellar expansion. It is not the most advanced colony, having relied on generation ships to bolster its population over a long period of time. However, its people have successfully terraformed two worlds, and live a simple lifestyle in one of the great agricultural experiments of the interstellar age. In 2268, scientists on Norma-36 F22b, "Rylos," detected a large band of unidentified bodies approaching from the outer system, some of which impacted the moon Yanto, knocking out the remote communications array on the moon's surface. Upon investigation, colonial engineers were attacked by a swarm of vicious bugs. This time, abandoning the moon was not an option, and the STAR marines were called in to cleanse the comms facility on Yanto. This was the first time a prepared force had taken

(OPPOSITE)
Winged Araknyds use their forelimbs to make slashing, hit-and-run attacks. They usually carry small explosive spore-bombs on their bodies, laying them like eggs as they soar over the battlefield.

NO-ONE WOULD HAVE BELIEVED...

Professor Harlan Forrester of the DSRS *Goodwill* was reputedly the first man to discover the nature of the Araknyd threat, though his work did not garner public attention until many months after the Lycea incident.

Forrester was one of the scientists tasked with studying Hell's Reach, using state-of-the-art astronomical equipment and relying largely on the data gathered from dozens of unmanned probes. Alone amongst his team, Forrester became convinced that an advanced form of life was present in the RSGC2 cluster – life-forms that were moving freely between the planets and moons of the region by riding upon meteorites and directing them on controlled trajectories through space. These observations were derided by the other researchers, who believed that the anomalous nature of the data was due to unidentified gravitational effects caused by the number of red super-giant stars in the sector.

Following the Lycea incident, Forrester was mysteriously reassigned to a top-secret facility back on Earth. His colleagues on the Goodwill station did not even get a chance to say goodbye before a squad of STAR marines bundled him away on board a military transport. What became of the professor – and what role he now fulfils in the STAR Industries scientific branch – remains a mystery.

---

on the bugs with the odds in their favor, and despite high casualty levels, the marines were ultimately successful. The marines' Demeter-class cruisers took out as many of the spore-meteorites as they could, although some were fired deeper coreward, beyond the sensor arrays of the colonies, headed for some unknown destination. Again, it seemed as though the Araknyds were working to some dire plan. In the years to come, battles would be fought on vast derelict ships, turned into little more than drifting hulks by the Araknyd meteors, and infested with hatchling bugs. The hulks themselves acted as transportation for the Araknyds, ultimately crashing into moons or barren worlds and unleashing an infestation of fully developed bugs onto previously untouched worlds. Since their discovery on Lycea, each new battle with the Araknyds shared a common feature – they were all closer to Earth than the last.

The idea of the Araknyds enacting some sort of vendetta against the human race quickly became the subject of a philosophical debate rather than a scientific one. No-one in the Authority wanted to believe that the first truly intelligent life encountered in the galaxy was a species of murderous, xenomorphic bug. However, any debate on the subject was soon to become moot.

Invasion: Earth

The war against the Araknyds raged throughout the galaxy, with new pockets of infestation being discovered on remote space stations, planetoids, and distant colonies throughout human territory. While the Authority dithered on exactly how to address the threat of a space-faring race of bugs, the reality of that threat came knocking at their door.

Five years ago, in 2283, the Araknyds' plan – if it can be called such – finally came to fruition. How long the spore-infested meteorites had been traveling towards the Sol system was unknown, but when a cluster of them, thousands strong, appeared on long-range sensors based in the asteroid belt, the domestic fleet was dispatched immediately. Made up of SolNav (the Sol system naval defense force) and the USD Coastguard, the fleet quickly identified the gigantic rocks as Araknyd spore-carriers, and quickly set about destroying them. Fragments of ice-bound rock scattered across the system, landing who-knows-where. Some of the meteorites made it through wholesale, and, after weeks of desperate action by the domestic fleet, five meteorites passed through the defense grid and impacted Earth.

Huge tidal waves crashed into the USA's western seaboard, while impact damage ravaged eastern Europe and parts of central Asia. The meteorites dispersed their deadly payload of tiny Araknyd spores instantly, poisoning the immediate atmosphere and rapidly evolving into Centauran warriors. Every STAR marine sortie within 12 light years was recalled to Earth, as the Terran Army and national defense forces struggled to contain the threat. By the time the STAR marines put down the threat, over 120 million citizens had been reported killed worldwide in the disaster. The world was united in its mourning, and searching questions were asked of the Authority. The response was a declaration of war on the Araknyds. Plans were put in place to expand the STAR Marine Corps, drafting in volunteers from the Army, Navy, and Coastguard, and even from colonial security forces. New training facilities were built; vast resources were diverted to STAR Industries' shipyards and weapon factories to bolster the fleet. Now, five years after the attempted invasion of Earth, one of the largest STAR Marine Corps task forces ever assembled is en route to the Centaurus Arm. Its mission – to find the source of the Araknyd threat, and erase it from the galaxy.

Combating the Threat

Perhaps the most difficult factor to overcome in actions against Araknyds is the aliens' ability to "terraform" the surrounding environment. The spores that herald the arrival of an infestation multiply rapidly, in a nano-biological attack on a planet's eco-system, blotting out the sun and slowly transforming the world into a barren, icy rock. Even after extensive clear-up operations on Earth, the areas most affected by the Araknyd invasion remain horribly polluted, with climate changing to arctic conditions and biological and radioactive contamination rife. Whenever Araknyds have gained a foothold on a world, they have instantly set about changing it to suit their needs, making the environment incredibly hostile for STAR marine operations.

Marine platoons fighting Araknyds are almost always accompanied by specialist teams equipped with flamethrowers, thermal detonators, and incendiary-loaded grenade launchers, as extreme heat appears to damage the creatures more than any other offensive measure. In mature Araknyd eco-systems, sealed environment suits are essential kit, to protect combatants from both

Known in the field as Hammerheads, these bugs are brutal monsters, larger and stronger than even an exo-suit marine.

atmospheric conditions and airborne bio-hazard. Close-quarter fighting against Araknyds is ill-advised; damage to environment suits exposes marines to a variety of fatal bacteria, while the creatures' strange plasma weaponry is devastating at close range. The Araknyds also use some form of synaptic feedback system both to communicate with each other and to receive orders from whatever intelligence guides the swarms – at close range this feedback can cause severe neural pain in humans, and sometimes incapacitation. In sub-zero conditions, exo-suits have proven unreliable, while dropsuit troopers are prone to engagement from vicious swarms of winged Araknyds and airborne explosive spores.

Thankfully the Araknyds do have other weaknesses that marine fireteams can exploit. Unlike Xeno-Parasites, Araknyds hunt mainly by sight, using motion-based vision in the thermal spectrum, as well as a form of bat-like echo-location – as such, thermal shielding and adaptive camouflage can conceal troopers from the bugs, especially at long range, while baffler grenades can sometimes cause mass confusion within a swarm. Anti-chitin ammunition has proven highly effective at stopping Araknyds when applied in mass volleys – using sentry gun emplacements to "herd" Araknyd swarms into the teeth of mass carbine volleys is one of the few tried and trusted tactics against Araknyd Warriors. Finally, Araknyds tend to lie dormant when a planet is at its hottest, hiding in vast subterranean burrows. Using pheromone traces extracted from slain bugs, anti-grav "smart nukes" have proven highly effective in penetrating these tunnel networks and detonating from within, often eradicating whole nests in the process.

Hive-Beasts of Klaatu VI

The Outer Arm of the galaxy has long been thought of as an untapped frontier – a vast stretch of systems, some almost certainly habitable, with untouched alien resources. Unfortunately, those worlds are located beyond some of the largest asteroid belts ever encountered, and so perilously close to unstable red giants and several black holes that FTL jumps along the Outer Arm are hazardous and sometimes deadly. For this reason, STAR Industries were reluctant to fully explore the outer reaches, leaving the way open for their competitors to seize the initiative, if only they could hold their nerve.

The first mega-corporation to successfully explore the fringe of the Outer Arm was Ramirez Hyperdrive, later renamed Cygnus AeroTech after a series of mergers with colonial mining corporations and military contractors. Their initial forays into the far reaches of the galaxy were rewarded when they colonized the Cygnus system – a venture so successful that the five terraformed planets are on the cusp of achieving Core World status.

The most lucrative expanse of space on the Outer Arm, however, was the sub-sector secreted within the vase Klaatu Nebula. From their newly established system, Cygnus AeroTech began to assemble an exploratory fleet that could negotiate this treacherous expanse and harvest the wealth of alien minerals that lay within it. This would, they hoped, acquire them power and wealth to finally rival STAR Industries. They poured resources into the project, risking almost everything to crack one of the largest unexplored regions of space. And they succeeded, up to a point.

Into the Nebula

The Klaatu Nebula is actually the critical region between several overlapping gaseous bodies, and is one of the largest nebulae in the Outer Arm. Cygnus

AeroTech, after several years of study, were able to navigate a path beyond the nebula, establishing a system of hyperspace beacons as they went, creating a safe path for future FTL jumps. This task took several years, but once completed it allowed manned expeditions into the systems beyond. What they found was a treasure trove of virgin worlds, ripe for the taking. The most promising system was named for the nebula itself – the Klaatu system – and long-range sensors had picked up high orichalcum, platinum, and thorium concentrations across the system, and identified at least two worlds in the habitable zones with water deposits. Before long massive mining and terraforming rigs were making their way towards the 12-planet system, light years ahead of any other corporation in what would surely become an interstellar gold-rush.

It was while conducting orbital examination of the super-giant Klaatu VI that a startling discovery was made, namely that the planet was not only ripe for terraforming, but also fostered alien life. Lessons of the past had taught mankind to proceed with caution in such circumstances, and eventually an endo-atmospheric exploration team was assembled to investigate the planet from the air, taking recordings and detailed scans as they went.

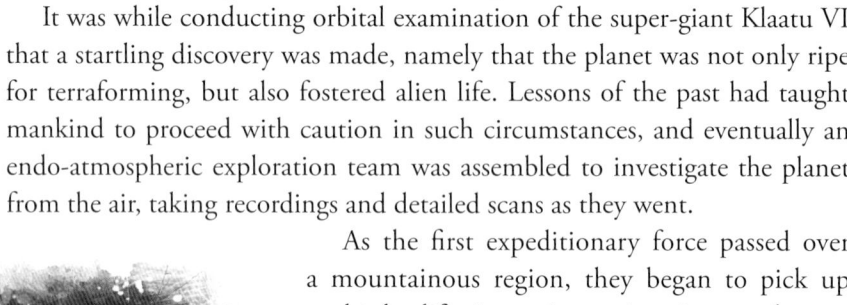

A recent battle on the fringe world of Remura confirmed a potentially new strain of 'Gun-Beast'. These large bugs fire gobbets of a napalm-like substance from their distended abdomens over incredible distances.

As the first expeditionary force passed over a mountainous region, they began to pick up multiple life-signs, increasing in number as the shuttle's altitude dropped. Sweeping lower for another pass through a steep valley, lined by towering, conical rock formations, the crew finally confirmed visual contact – bugs. This news was met with utter dismay by the orbiting command vessel – contact with alien bugs prior to that point had never gone well, and these ones looked no better. They were akin to large crustaceans, scuttling about the mountainsides in droves, eyestalks waving and claws snapping in the air at the shuttle's approach. The exploratory mission was recalled, and the shuttle began its ascent – and that's when things took a turn for the worse.

As the shuttle climbed passed the strange conical mountain peaks, the crew noticed hundreds of small caves pock-marking the surface of the rock. From these, clouds of flying bugs began to swarm, and, too late, the crew realized that the mountains were not truly mountains at all, but gigantic nests harboring the strange aliens of Klaatu VI – bug-built structures resembling cyclopean termite mounds.

The creatures swarmed the shuttle, clogging the engines in thickening waves, until finally the crew were forced to crash land further along the valley floor. A distress beacon was erected, and the command ship, ATSS *Compass Rose*, received a brief transmission informing them that the shuttle crew were heading north, away from the mountainous hives.

Following standard protocol, the *Compass Rose* immediately sent word to the nearest STAR marine company, operating some 2,000 light years away. The *Compass Rose* sent full clearance to allow the marines to use their newly laid beacon network, and waited. The unthinkable happened – after checking in with STAR Command, the marines refused to respond. Thousands of light years away, via light-squeezed transmissions, a tense round of corporate negotiations began between STAR Industries and Cygnus AeroTech, in which STAR refused to send their marines into rival corporate territory without first agreeing a contract with an astronomical remuneration clause. The talks came to a standstill, at which point the captain of the *Compass Rose*, Helena Bergstrom, took matters into her own hands and organized a security detail to rescue the shuttle crew.

Landing an estimated safe distance from the hives and encountering minimal hostiles, the security detail set about tracking the shuttle crew, eventually tracing their ID blips to a remote crystal stalagmite forest. This in itself was of great interest to the landing party, who gathered a few samples of the strange rock before continuing their mission.

Finally, the ID blips led the security detail to a range of low hills, and a deep burrow where the shuttle crew had evidently crawled. With no comms response, the detail had little option but to investigate. Deep below ground, they found four survivors of the recon shuttle crew, their eyes strange and white, their minds seemingly useless. They twitched and moaned like zombies, and seemed to have lost all control of their higher functions. The security detail were about to carry the crewmen bodily from the cave when they were disturbed by a violent tremor from deeper below ground. A huge sinkhole opened in the center of the chamber, and a massive bug erupted through it – a larval, worm-like creature, at least 13 feet in diameter, with a gaping mouth filled with row after row of razor-sharp teeth. As soon as the first shots were fired, the creature emitted a high-pitched squeal that caused massive hemorrhaging in the closest men, forcing the remainder to flee the scene. From every side-tunnel, large, crab-like monsters scuttled out in pursuit, and after a running firefight with the creatures only two men made it back to the retrieval boat alive. As the suns dropped below the horizon, the entire planet seemed to spring alive with scuttling black shapes. The retrieval boat jetted away, shooting its way through a storm of flying crustaceans, and returning badly damaged to the *Compass Rose,* with a skeleton crew.

Captain Bergstrom had barely relayed news of the bizarre ambush by the bugs when her ship went into red alert. In minutes, fires raged across the

vessel, and gunfire sounded in every corridor. The returning retrieval boat had brought with it deadly cargo – reddish ooze stuck to the hull, in which writhed hundreds of small, psychic larvae. Wriggling their way into the ship, they crawled into the ears and noses of sleeping crewmen, hijacking their neural functions and turning them against their comrades. These bug-controlled crewmen quickly began to transmit the horrific alien virus to their colleagues, vomiting worm-infested blood onto uncontaminated crew and bringing them swiftly under their synaptic control. Within an hour, the ship's destruct sequence had been activated, and detonated, blasting the *Compass Rose* in half and sending the huge vessel crashing to the surface of Klaatu VI in flames.

Let the Bug Hunt Commence

With the loss of the *Compass Rose*, Cygnus AeroTech lost heart in their negotiations with STAR Industries. STAR, on the other hand, were even more determined to wrest additional mining rights in the Klaatu system from Cygnus, as the discovery of the strange crystal mineral on the planet's surface represented a sizeable scientific and fiscal opportunity. And so finally Cygnus relented, giving up valuable mining rights, and at long last the STAR marines were dispatched to the Klaatu Nebula – four full expeditionary units, including two from the famous 5th Arcturian Regiment, were sent with a list of prioritized standing orders: retrieve samples of the crystalline rock, capture a bug specimen for further study, and search the planet for survivors of the *Compass Rose*.

The marines touched down just two klicks from the *Compass* Rose's tail section, and instantly set up firebases and field HQ. Three platoons were sent towards the wreckage in Armored Personnel Carriers (APCs), following the plumes of smoke that still smoldered a week after the crash. The remaining marines were split into patrols to search the surrounding landscape for mineral deposits and enemy activity.

Heading northeast towards the original contact site, it was two platoons of the Arcturian 5th that first encountered hostiles. Skirting the perimeter of the smallest hive-zone, they'd hoped to go undetected, but the heavy wheels of their Timberwolf APCs created enough ground disturbance to attract unwelcome attention. The large, crab-like bugs described by the exploration party scuttled from every cave-mouth, massive claws snapping in the air as they bore down on the marines. Carbine-fire bounced off the bugs' thick, patterned carapaces. Grenades, although effective at slowing the bugs down, only seemed to attract more of their ilk as the explosions tore through the earth. As the intensity of the swarm increased, the marines fell back to their APCs and sped away from the mounds as fast as they could, eventually outstripping the bugs for speed. Unfortunately, they didn't get far before a seismic disturbance ahead caused the APCs to ditch. A smaller bug patrol climbed from the newly opened fissure and began to smash into the

(OPPOSITE)
Soldier-Beasts are large and powerful, a mass of talons, mandibles and crushing claws, protected by a thick carapace. They are carrion feeders, and can often be found clearing battlefields of the dead – both their own and the enemy's.

APCs, battering them with their massive chitinous shoulders and tearing at them with huge crab-like claws. Uncertain of how long the APCs' armor would hold, the marine specialists on board donned powered exo-suits and deployed outside, taking the fight to the bugs.

While one exo-suit specialist set about righting the APCs, the other three waded into close-quarter combat against the aliens. With their power-assisted servos, the exo-suit troopers proved the physical equal of the bugs, while their inbuilt flamethrowers, carbines, and grenade packs made up for their lack of numbers. The bugs' massive claws proved capable of tearing through exo-suit armor plating, but the marines' combat training gave them the tactical advantage. Three suits stood against more than 20 bugs, desperately buying their platoon enough time to get underway. Only once the APCs were good to go did the exo-suit specialists disengage, one of them irreparably damaged. Fire support troopers wielding heavy auto-carbines and railguns – the only weapons capable of penetrating the crab-beasts' thick chitin armor – laid down covering fire. Even as the marines got underway and left the bugs behind, the sky behind them began to darken as swarms of flying aliens flocked from the distant hives. The beasts were nothing if not tenacious.

Elsewhere, the other platoons were also running into trouble. At the wreckage of the *Compass Rose*, three platoons drawn from the 3rd and 7th Magellan regiments forced their way into the huge sundered vessel. Picking their way through the dark, twisted corridors of the wreck, the fireteams picked up multiple vital signs from somewhere near the reactor room. Upon approach, a group of crewmen in engineering uniforms stumbled from the darkness towards them. The first fireteam attempted to escort the survivors to safety, realizing too late that they were no longer fully human, but were instead infected with virulent worm-hatchlings. The crew shambled forward, rapidly followed by more, who had previously been thought dead. Soon, every corpse in the engineering section was climbing to its feet and attacking the marines.

The marines on point were quickly overwhelmed – the press of bodies piled onto them, vomiting black blood over them. Unable to tell if any of the remaining life-signs were from genuine survivors or infected, Corporal Zander of the 7th Magellan gave the order to pull back. Retreating in good order, the marines quickly found that carbine fire did little to stop the infected crew unless direct head-shots were scored. Flamethrowers were brought up to the front, and any marine carrying a shotgun or frag pistol moved to the rear to blast apart their pursuers.

Outside, the marines realized that they'd been treading through hazardous material, likely containing microscopic bug larvae. That they were carrying parasitic organisms on their persons became the least of their worries, however, as larger, fatter larvae began to wriggle from the storeys-high wreckage, forcing their fat bodies from every hatch and crevice until they rained down onto the

(OPPOSITE)
Worker-Beasts, dubbed 'death-shrimps' by marines, are the builders of the gigantic hives in which their species lives. Akin to gigantic hornets, or winged shrimps, their tails are tipped with a wasp-like sting, capable of injecting one of the most virulent neuro-toxins ever encountered by mankind.

marines. Those stationed outside opened fire, but many of the larvae burrowed quickly underground only to re-emerge beneath the marines' feet, biting through their fatigues with razor-sharp fangs. The marines scrambled back to their APCs in disarray, firing at a writhing mass of tunneler worms as they went. The crew, now zombies in thrall to the bugs, staggered from the ruins, throwing themselves onto the APCs. Worse still, the marines who had been lost inside the wreckage also emerged, their eyes white, firing their weapons at former comrades. With men down, and a serious risk of contamination, the marines high-tailed it back to the firebase.

It was the same for every patrol. The bugs had attacked anyone who had drawn close to their territory, driving them off with overwhelming numbers, and finally pursuing them across the rocky steppe. At the firebase, the marines regrouped in time to see bugs scurrying across the plain from every direction, and tens of thousands more approaching from the air. The marines set up long-ranged emplacements and fired relentlessly into the swarms while they waiting for air support to pick them up. As they fought, their own wounded began to turn, attacking them from within the base. As the battle raged, Corporal Zander found himself the most senior officer in the expedition, and gave the order to withdraw, leaving any wounded behind and abandoning masses of hardware.

Infection

Back on board the cruisers, the medical teams worked around the clock to quarantine and screen every marine who had been planetside. Some quickly developed second-stage infections and were frozen in cryo-sleep to stop the alien virus from spreading. Any gear that had come into contact with the strange, worm-infested ooze was fired out of an airlock. Three Demeter-class cruisers full of potentially infected marines were sent back to the nearest STAR Command facility for further study, while one – the MSS *Mako* – remained to patrol the sector, forming a temporary Star Marine Expeditionary Unit (SMEU) from the surviving marines.

The STAR science and tech division discovered that the infectious larvae begin as microscopic organisms, and quickly grow into caterpillar-sized grubs. Those that do not find a host body to control continue to grow, until eventually they reach prodigious size – they are undoubtedly the same strain as the large tunneling worms encountered by the Cygnus exploration team. The creatures are aggressive and intelligent, displaying a strong sense of self-preservation. When they reach larger sizes, their ability to control biological organisms becomes remote – a psychic ability that intensifies the older the bug becomes. At adult stage, they quickly turn on each other, devouring their kin in order to grow stronger and, it is theorized, start their own hive. These bugs, although completely androgynous, were dubbed Queen-Beasts, and their species became known as Hive-Beasts (*Xeno Praesepes Bellua*).

REVENANT SLAVE-HOSTS

The most terrifying aspect of facing the Hive-Beasts of Klaatu VI is their ability to turn marine against marine, and take full control of a human's neural processes. At a basic level, this control is asserted through infection with the aliens' blood or specially secreted synaptic fluid. These fluids contain tens of thousands of parasitic worms, which are the first stages in the development of the Queen-Beasts. As these worms enter the bloodstream, they take full control of the host's hemocoel, flooding the body with neural suppressants, in turn allowing the parasites to latch onto the dorsal root ganglia and take complete control of a person's bodily functions. If allowed to grow outside of a host body, the microscopic worms soon become small grubs, themselves able to burrow into a victim and pump more micro-parasites into the host's system. Although the "brainworms" are not in themselves intelligent until they reach full maturity, they use their powers to induct a victim into the nest's "hive mind," forcing the host to act to defend the hive at all costs.

The host, while unable to access memories or even feel pain under the influence of the brainworms, does seem to pass on knowledge and training to the hive mind – psychically "possessed" marines can utilize all of their equipment and weaponry, albeit clumsily, while spacecraft pilots have even been forced to ditch their vessels into marine convoys by the pernicious hive mind.

A Rock and a Hard Place

Analysis of the various mineral deposits retrieved from Klaatu VI revealed high concentrations of crystallized thorium – one of the essential elements required to power hyperdrive engines – as well as rich seams of platinum, titanium, and orichalcum ore within the planet's rock formations. Study of the Hive-Beasts' carcasses led STAR scientists to postulate that the pure elements were a by-product of the bugs' tunneling activities – the process of chewing out their vast nests creates a wealth of minerals that are completely useless to the bugs, but incredibly valuable to humans. If STAR Industries could find a way to exploit the bugs' natural tendencies, the potential would be limitless. However, the Hive-Beasts were highly aggressive and highly organized, and represented a potentially disastrous bio-hazard threat.

In the following months, further exploration of the Klaatu Nebula and the surrounding sectors led to a disturbing discovery. The Hive-Beasts were not limited to Klaatu VI, but had spread to well over a dozen worlds, as well as mustering a complete infestation of the Klaatuan asteroid belt. Meteorites displaying strange, conical formations on their surfaces were seen hurtling through the sector, seemingly at random. Like the Centauran Araknyds, the Hive-Beasts had found a way to spread beyond their homeworld – wherever that might be. Unlike the Araknyds, however, their expansion appeared utterly random. Where their meteorite burrows crashed, they made their home. Where their spores infected another race, they spread like wildfire. There was no telling how many infested worlds there were, or how far-reaching their territory – but given the valuable resources that the aliens possessed, war with the Hive-Beasts would be inevitable.

STAR Industries' initial refusal to assist the Cygnus system on the grounds of conflict of interests ultimately persuaded the Authority to take sanctions against their previously benevolent corporate saviors. The Pan-System Concordance of 2271 signed over greater control of the STAR Marine Corps to the Authority, and forbade STAR Industries from profiting directly from marine deployments beyond the lucrative defense contract already in place. By that time, however, the damage to Cygnus AeroTech had been done, and the corporation became little more than a large subsidiary of STAR Industries in the ensuing years.

All-out War

In the meantime, however, STAR Industries set about securing the Klaatu sector, sending every available marine patrol through the nebula. Their plan was to secure the system, and construct their own sanctioned hyperlane jump-gate in orbit around Klaatu VI. The system, and undoubtedly much of the sector beyond it, was too valuable to allow another upstart company like Cygnus to move in, and so STAR set about conducting the largest ground offensive in its history. Two full regiments of STAR marines moved into the region, supported by a SolNav carrier and five companies of Terran Army soldiers. In order to save as much of the mineral wealth of the planet as possible, orbital nukes were prohibited, and so the troops, under General Ansom B. Valentine of the 5th Arcturians, prepared for a lengthy ground war.

The campaign lasted for over a year, during which the STAR marines were reinforced several times. At first, the marines' tactics were woefully deficient, and despite their bravery many marines were infected by alien parasites and became little more than slavering revenants, fighting against their own people. The war raged across deserts, and in the bowels of the hives themselves. With each battle lost, the marines adapted and learned new tactics. Every man killed or possessed taught the STAR scientists something new about the bugs of Klaatu VI – and how to kill them. Inch by inch, the marines made ground. When the first Queen-Beast was killed, the effect on the surrounding bugs was dramatic – they became confused and docile, and easy to put down. Though there were perhaps 20 more hives scattered across the planet's primary continent, each containing billions of bugs, this victory gave the marines heart. They burned the dead – revenant, marine, and bug alike – regrouped, rearmed, and moved onto the next hive. By the time the last hive fell, every surviving soldier on the planet was a hardened veteran. But there was no time to rest – similar wars were being fought across the sector, and while the engineers moved in to begin terraforming Klaatu VI, the marines and Terran Army moved out to the next dropzone. This would be the way of it for years to come…

(OPPOSITE)
Queen-Beasts are massive, tunnelling creatures. There are several of these beasts to be found in any one hive complex, each directing a horde of smaller creatures with an almost psionic control method.

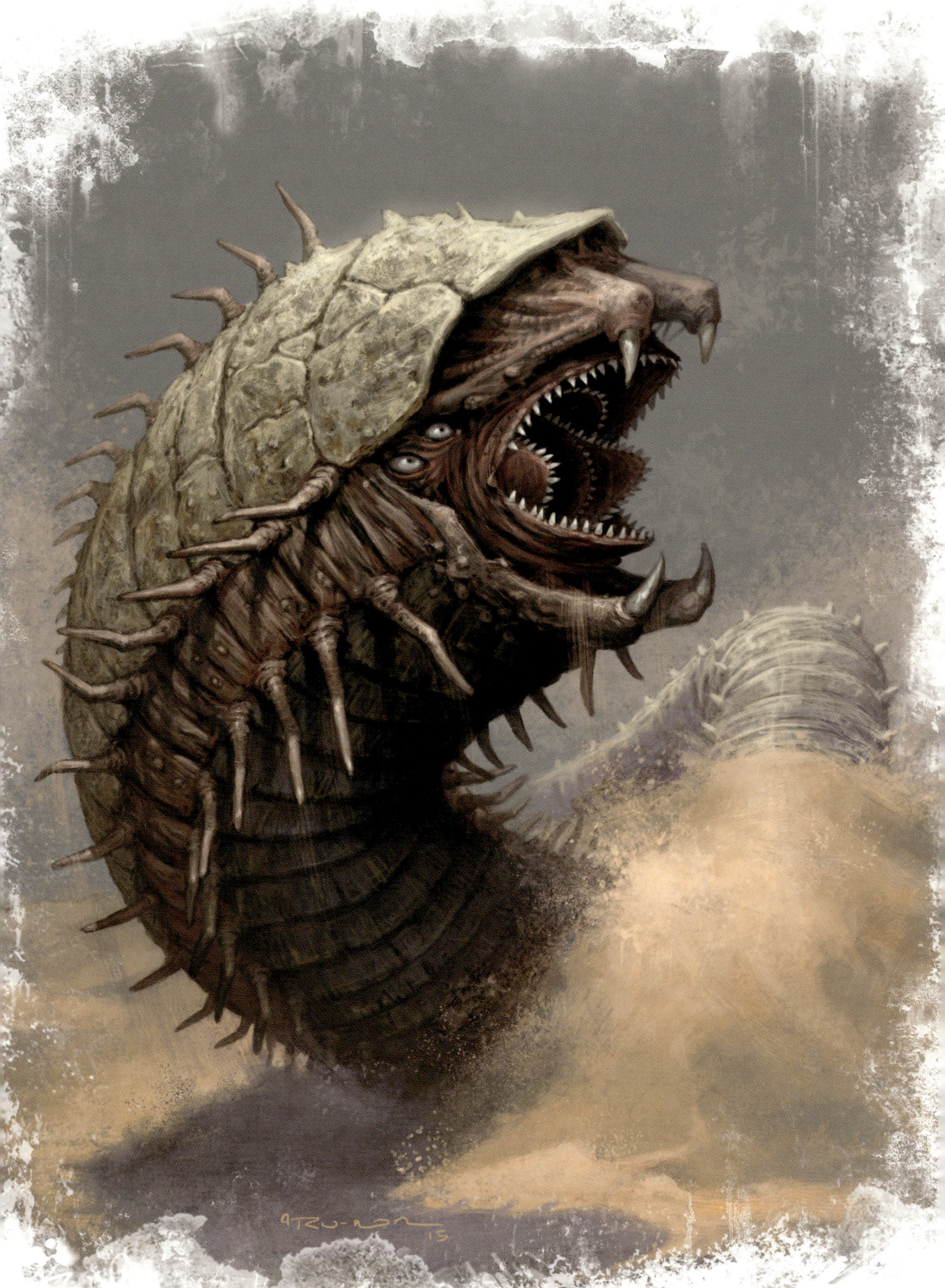

Combating the Threat

Engaging Hive-Beasts at close range is incredibly hazardous. Their crab-like Soldier-Beasts are large and powerful, and incredibly aggressive, especially when defending their hives. Air support, and particularly the use of personal dropsuits, is made difficult by the swarms of Worker-Beasts, which flock together in huge numbers during battle. If there is no option but to get in close, marines are prescribed the use of sealed environment armor, while specialists are usually equipped with exo-suits, which have proven the physical equal of the larger bugs. At range, railguns are the weapon of choice – of all bug species encountered so far, Hive-Beast Soldiers have the thickest exo-skeletons – almost like heavy shells. Railguns offer superior armor penetration and range – though they are often in short supply.

The use of "nestbuster" smart nukes has had limited success on several Hive-Beast infestations, but given the sheer size of the larger nests they do not always possess the range to take down the hive's Queen-Beast. The only sure-fire way of scattering a hive is by destroying this Queen and any juveniles, which almost always means sending a patrol deep into a hive to take down the creature at close quarters. This method presents many dangers. Firstly, the risk of infection is high, as deposits of worm-infested goo drop from every surface inside the hives. Once an environment suit is compromised and a marine is infected, he has only minutes before he falls under the control of the Hive-Beasts. Secondly, fighting Soldier-Beasts at close quarters is incredibly dangerous, even with the use of anti-chitin shotgun rounds and flamethrowers. Thirdly, within the nests, every vibration is amplified, and the bugs seem particularly sensitive to intruders, much like Earth spiders and their webs. Finally, the Queen-Beast herself, as well as being surrounded by vicious workers and voracious larvae, is capable of activating remote psionic control of individual marines or even small groups, turning fireteams against each other even without the aid of her "brainworm" spore.

Only six "Queen-hunts" have ever been attempted, and only one of those was successful. When the Queen-Beast was destroyed and her larvae put to the torch, all of the other bugs from the hive began to wander aimlessly, in a confused state, and were easily defeated. Two recent innovations, however, have made the prospect of Queen-hunts less of a suicide mission and more of a tactical possibility. Firstly, a pheromone spray applied to the marines' fatigues masks their presence to the bugs' heightened scent receptors, meaning that the Hive-Beasts must actually see the marines in order to detect them, and can thus be picked off piecemeal before organizing a stiff resistance. Secondly, some headway has been made into the development of neural-dampener drugs. Unlike other combat drugs, these are designed specifically to block those neural receptors that the Queen-Beasts try to exploit, making it much harder to "possess" an injected marine. However, the side-effects can be severe, with some marines reporting severe headaches and slowed reaction times in the field.

Bugs of the Galaxy

The 5th Arcturian Regiment gets all the glory, 'cos they're the meanest hombres in the galaxy. We call 'em the "Bravos" – short for "Bravo-Sierra," or "Bug Stompers." We say Bravos 'cos they don't like being called the BS Regiment. It's best not to get on their bad side – if they even have a good side, that is.

– Sergeant Marquez, 12th Lunar Regiment

Since the first hostile alien organisms were discovered more than 60 years ago, more than 20 distinct species have been cataloged, all of which have fallen more or less under the broad categorization of "bugs." From tiny, poisonous insects to massive, hundred-legged arthropods, all bugs seem to share an innate hatred of human life. Mankind has all but given up hope of finding any truly intelligent life in the galaxy – and if there ever was a great civilization, surely the bugs would have wiped them out by now! Beyond the three main strains of alien bug so far encountered, the following are also worthy of note.

Crab Beasts of Triton

Xeno Carcino Brutus

One of the first strains of bug to be discovered, the so-called "crab-beasts" were at first thought to be small, generally harmless crustaceans, much like the blue crabs of Earth. Terraformers and miners running surveys on the surface of Triton (Neptune's largest moon) were intrigued by the creatures, which displayed the peculiar defense mechanism of disguising themselves as rocks. Whilst carrying out excavations beneath Triton's frozen surface, the miners discovered larger crabs, considerably older and more gnarled than those above ground. Although these creatures were more aggressive than their diminutive surface cousins, they were still too small to prove a real threat, and were soon scared away by the team's security officer. A few days later, however, when delving deeper into the moon's rocky core, the miners disturbed a nest of even larger creatures – this time highly aggressive and almost as big as a man. Several miners were killed as the "crab-beasts" surfaced, and Triton's colonists engaged in battles against the monsters that lasted for weeks. When Earth's media got hold of the story, "bug-mania" began to sweep the solar system, and the army was dispatched to save face. The mining colonies still exist on Triton, and still occasionally fend off attacks from small nests of crab-beasts. The only thing scientists have yet to figure out is why the creatures have the ability to disguise themselves – there appears to be no other life on the moon, so what did they evolve to hide from?

A STAR marine of the famous 5th Arcturian regiment armed with combi-carbine, laying down suppressing fire.

Europan Ice-Squid
Xeno Rhomboteuthis Europa

The smallest of Jupiter's four "Galilean" moons, Europa is a ball of ice-covered rock that has long been believed to harbor primitive life. In 2214, core samples taken from the ice by a lunar rover uncovered the unmistakable signs of bacterial life, though dormant on the samples recovered. A manned flight to Europa touched down in 2219, consisting of a six-man xeno-biologist team with sophisticated drilling and sampling equipment. During the course of their seven-day surface mission, the team were apparently attacked by a squid-like creature, which lured them to thin ice by means of its bio-luminescent properties. The attack led to ruptures in the ice, and ultimately the loss of the entire mission. Grainy images of the "rhomboteuthis" made it back to the Authority, and some were leaked to the media, though they were quickly discredited. It is unknown whether further missions ever returned to Europa.

Tuomi Arthropods
Xeno Pedis Armenta

The only example to date of an alien life-form that has been subjugated by humans, the oxen-sized arthropods of the super-Earth, Tuomi, were initially thought to be a severe threat to the foundling civilian colony on the planet, and were culled with extreme prejudice. Although naturally aggressive, especially when raising young, the arthropods were soon found to be rather stupid and docile when left alone. After experimenting on several specimens, STAR's HD 10180 fringe science division managed to attach crude neural inhibitors to the creatures' brain stems, affording them a measure of control over the arthropods' movements. In addition, the flesh of the creatures was found to be fit for human consumption and rich in protein and minerals, while the outer carapace provided excellent material for ballistic testing and marine training. The Tuomi arthropods can now be found across human territory, where they are used as both pack animals and cattle.

Antares Gorgons
Xeno Cyanea Medusa

First discovered on the volcanic world of Masu Sar in the Antares system, the Gorgons are one of the strangest alien species ever identified. Due to the extreme conditions on their homeworlds – a trio of hot worlds closest to their red super-giant star – close observation has been difficult, although a detachment of STAR marines was once called upon to protect a manned exploration mission from the attentions of these bizarre creatures. They are certainly sentient, and aggressive, although they usually ignore other beings as long as they don't get too close.

Essentially a type of polyp, similar in biology to a Portuguese man o'war, the Gorgons are large, floating, gaseous jellyfish that drift on thin thermal currents across their planets, seemingly drawn to volcanic activity. Their bloated, translucent bodies grow up to 16 feet in diameter, and are covered with large orbs – possibly sensory organs – and tiny, waving tentacles that they use to "steer" themselves. Dozens of tendrils trail along beneath them, sometimes 50 yards in length; these appear to collect small pieces of basalt, which the Gorgon then feeds into its beak-like mouth and breaks down into constituent minerals.

Once per Antares year, the Gorgons flock together for a mass migration, where they cross the great inert wastes on the planet's equator to reach the next hemisphere in time for the surface's warming. They prepare for this great feat by drifting high into the thin atmosphere and creating an electrical storm

Fossilised remains of long-dead bugs are found all over the galaxy, suggesting that these monsters have been around for a long time.

using their own bio-electric energy. Lightning crackles within and without the creatures' bodies, dancing around their flowing tendrils, and giving them the power to drift across the 3,000-mile plains. The sight of this exodus from space is beautiful, but also disturbing – this method is surely how the creatures managed to migrate to other planets in their solar system, meaning that they can not only survive in space, but also direct themselves to a suitable world.

Talahassium Gronks
Xeno Macero Proboscis

The pulsar star at the heart of the Crab Nebula is orbited by seven planets, three of which are made up of almost pure illyrium, a key component in super-miniaturized computer processors. Exploration of this system is incredibly hazardous given the unpredictable emissions from the star, but a shielded hyperspace jump-gate was constructed in orbit around one of the worlds – Talahassium II. Given its location, composition, and tenuous atmosphere, the discovery of life on that world was thought utterly impossible – but the rules of human science have a way of being contradicted in the cold depths of space.

When STAR engineers attempted to construct a hyperspace booster on the planet's surface, they were attacked by a pack of large, lumbering creatures which would later become known by the nickname "gronks." Roughly the size and bulk of the Terran hippopotamus, but shaped more like a toad, these smooth-skinned, gray-white creatures have the bizarre ability to expand and contort their elastic bodies at will. Gronks possess no eyes, but instead feel their way around with a cluster of sensitive tentacles on the end of their snout. Their vast mouths have no teeth, but their feet are tipped with large claws, used for prizing the soft innards from another Talahassium native, the Illyrium Clam. Unfortunately for the first humans to set foot on the planet, gronks aren't too picky about what they eat; they swallowed two engineers whole before the rest were able to escape and call in the marines.

Today, Talahassium II is home to several illyrium auto-rigs, which harvest the valuable minerals from the ground and send it off-world via a space elevator to a waiting unmanned station. Once every six Earth months, when the pulsar star is relatively stable, a freighter arrives through the jump-gate to collect the latest shipment. Needless to say, whenever an engineer team is required to go planetside for maintenance, it is always accompanied by a squad of STAR marines.

The Gehenna Remnants

Orbiting the unstable Mu Cephei super-giant, the planet Gehenna is a world of purple ash deserts, strange blue-black crystal forests, and towering obsidian mountains. It has long been a site for STAR Industries deep science research, given the unique conditions in which the planet exists and the strange and varied landscape they have created. Many scientific advances from the last 50 years have come about as a direct result of studying Gehenna and its neighboring worlds.

One discovery from Gehenna not to make the public eye was evidence of the past existence of life on the planet. Beneath the shifting purple desert, astro-geologists uncovered evidence of complex structures made of naturally grown crystal. Initially, it was thought that these structures were created through random chance, but the discovery of more of these "sites of interest" soon convinced the scientists that they were the product of intelligent design. More recently, fossilized remains of alien life-forms have been unearthed, which were immediately dispatched to STAR's fringe science division for further study. The fossils were of crustaceous beings, about 5 feet long, with large membranous wings and several sets of articulate limbs. Atop their beaked heads were large, human-like brains. Most disturbingly, the scientists found evidence of strange tools and even weapons, all grown from native crystals, and now long-inert. These artefacts, and the fossils themselves, dated back over five million years. What happened to this strange alien race, and just how intelligent they were, remains to be seen. But their existence remains a closely guarded secret – after all, who on Earth would really want to know that the only ancient civilization discovered in the entire galaxy was itself a race of ugly bugs?

INFAMOUS INFESTATIONS — A TIMELINE OF BUG HUNTS

For almost 50 years, the Pan-System Marine Corps has done two things for the advancement of mankind: make marines, and squash bugs.
– Colonel Abraham T. Stokeley, 5th Arcturian Regiment, STAR Pan-System Marine Corps

2070
The mega-corporation Stellar Dynamic patents the first reliable sub-light stardrive, capable of propelling manned vessels at a little below the speed of light, using advanced particle engines.

2086
After early teething problems, artificial intelligence super-processors are developed to plot safe courses for sub-light vessels, making in-flight adjustments for extra-terrestrial hazards that a human could not.

2098
Research colonies are established on Mars and Titan. The first extra-orbital space stations are built near the moons Titan, Io, and Triton. Rumors of the discovery of small, crab-like creatures on Triton are quashed.

2116
First manned flights beyond the solar system achieved. Mission Gagarin sends an international team to Alpha Centauri, while Mission Aldrin does the same for Tau Ceti. The trips are one-way.

2119
The mega-corporation Ark Industries completes the first generation ship, and sends it to Alpha Centauri, overshadowing Stellar Dynamic's achievements. The project sends 100 souls into space, with enough equipment to be fully self-sustaining, and to make a ground-based colony on the surface of Centauri B.

2124

Professor Hans Falken, president of Ark Industries, is awarded a seat on the United Nations Council – the first corporate figure to be handed full governmental powers.

2136

First light-squeezed transmission received from the Alpha Centauri system, proving that the research party made it alive and well.

2169

Even as the first generation ship colony begins to build structures on Centauri B, and with another generation ship en route to Tau Ceti, Stellar Dynamic

Only encountered once, on the lush jungle-world of Lenticulus V, these massive creatures known as 'super-spiders' are the largest bug strain ever encountered.

unveils its hypersleep technology, making the idea of generation ships obsolete. Highly trained individuals are now able to travel in suspended animation for a maximum of 30-year stretches during long voyages.

2210
Ark Industries initiates a hostile takeover of Stellar Dynamic in a bid to accelerate its manufacture of faster-than-light starships. The new mega-corp, STAR Industries, owns almost a tenth of Earth's wealth, and uses resources mined from deep-space colonies to build ships and space stations off-world.

2214
Simple-celled alien organisms are discovered on over a dozen planets and moons, giving hope that there may be intelligent life out there in the galaxy. STAR Industries begins to work with the newly formed United Nations Authority to plot exploratory missions to the outer arms of the Milky Way.

2227
The Lunar Incursion. Whilst excavating a network of subterranean caves beneath Triton's surface, the semi-permanent research colony uncovers a nest of crustaceous aliens. Though mostly small and easily subdued, the oldest and largest beasts kill several miners before the security forces can reach them. Evidence of the "Crab-beasts of Triton" is finally uncovered by Earth's media.

2234
Humanity reaches a milestone of 100 thriving deep-space colonies, covering 24 systems. The human population in the galaxy is at an all-time high. The United Nations Authority becomes the Pan-System Authority to recognize the growing democratic rights of off-world colonies.

2239
A scientific expedition is launched on Draper's World in the HD 40307 system. After weeks of working on the surface, the scientists encounter an aggressive alien life form, and retreat to the nearest space station, the Kepler facility. There, the first "bugs" are identified, labeled simply the Draper's World Xeno-Parasite.

2241
STAR Industries wins the bid to privatize interstellar defense. Over the next five years, contracts with two other military hardware mega-corporations are drawn up, and the formalized STAR Pan-System Marine Corps is born.

2245
Bacteria discovered on Jupiter's volcanic moon, Io, infect the scientists on board the moon's orbital research station. All 39 crew are wiped out by parasites, which use the scientists' bodies as hosts. STAR marines are dispatched to wipe out the threat, and identify the bugs as the Draper's World strain. Unable to save the station, they eventually destroy it with railgun fire from their carrier. How the Xeno-Parasites reached Io remains a mystery – or a closely guarded secret.

2246
A fringe exploratory fleet near RSGC2 (aka Hell's Reach) in the Centaurus galactic arm discovers life signs on two ice-bound planetoids. Investigation reveals a highly aggressive race, driven by an almost psychic intelligence. Nicknamed the "Araknyds," when these bugs display the ability to leave their worlds and pursue the humans through space, the research facilities are abandoned.

2248
A STAR marine platoon engages Xeno-Parasites on the ice world Perdition. By sacrificing the surviving colonists, the marines are able to engage the bugs on an open battlefield, scoring a complete victory over the insidious Xeno-Parasites.

2253
STAR marines successfully stamp out the threat posed by aggressive arthropods on the "super-Earth" Tuomi in the HD 10180 system. The creatures are later subjugated by the use of fringe-science neural inhibitors, and shipped to colonies across the galaxy as hardy draft animals, being able to survive in virtually any atmosphere.

2268
Centauran Araknyds are found in the Scutum Reaches, and later on the moon Yanto, in the Norma-36 system. Theories are postulated that the Araknyds, having made an enemy of humans, are moving through the galaxy purposefully, drawing nearer to the solar system with each passing day. Such theories are laughed off.

2270
The first mass land war is fought between humans and bugs. A new bug species, controlled by a hive mind nexus, is discovered in the Klaatu Nebula. As this is seen as the gateway to a mineral-rich system, and a prime location for a hyperlane jump-gate, STAR Industries sends two regiments of marines to protect human interests in the region.

2271

The population of the agricultural colony on Kepler-62e reaches 10,000. After the discovery of Xeno-Parasites on the neighboring giant planet 62f, a permanent orbital defense station is built around the colonial world, with a standing garrison of one marine company, a deep space naval launch platform, and associated hardware.

2283

A huge meteor shower hits Earth. Although defense platforms break up most of the gigantic rocks before they enter orbit, several pound the planet, releasing an Araknyd threat onto Terran soil. By the time the Authority's territorial military put down the threat, over 120 million citizens have been killed.

2288 (the present)

Training of STAR marines is accelerated as the threat to the core worlds of human colonization grows. A strong marine fleet is sent to explore the fringes of the Centaurus Arm, to locate the homeworld of the Araknyds in preparation for a full-scale assault.

STAR INDUSTRIES AND THE PAN-SYSTEM MARINE CORPS

You can have your Groundhog Khakis,
And your SolNav Blues,
But here's a different fighting man,
I'll introduce to you.
His uniform is unlike
Any you've ever seen,
The Bugs think he's the Devil born,
His title is 'Marine'.

– STAR Marine Cadence

Mankind's primary interstellar defense force, the STAR marines are also the first military force to be fully privatized, owned, and equipped by the galactic mega-corporation, STAR Industries. The relationship between the Pan-System Authority and STAR Command is not always harmonious. Ultimately, much of the funding for the Marine Corps comes from the Authority's contract with STAR, but on several occasions STAR have hesitated – or even refused – to deploy the marines when doing so would prove counter to their corporate interests. If it weren't for STAR's CEO occupying his traditional seat on the ruling council, the sanctions for this disobedience could have been severe. In truth, although STAR need full government backing to operate as they do, they have reached the point where their corporate wealth outstrips the GDP of 50 per cent of the core worlds combined – and with that amount of power of their disposal, they become increasingly difficult to control.

In the eyes of the general public, the STAR marines can do no wrong. STAR's 24-7 Bug Hunts holovision channel broadcasts across 90 worlds, and no HV show is more popular than the fly-on-the-wall *Arcturian Wars*. Heavily edited (and, some suggest, even fabricated), the show follows the exploits of pretty STAR marine poster-girl Captain Ana Carter and her legendary Zero Platoon, as they stomp bugs in warzones across the galaxy. Branding and promotion is all-important to STAR – Ana Carter action figures are one of the highest-selling products in the galaxy, and more men and women sign up to the Marine Corps after each Arcturian Wars broadcast than at any other time. Such is the way of the galaxy that the STAR marines are not just mankind's best hope for defense against the alien hordes, but also valuable commodities to be bought and sold.

For STAR Industries, the Araknyd invasion of Earth couldn't have come at a better time. Several high-profile disagreements between STAR and the Authority had threatened to derail renegotiation of the defense contract. However, the wave of Core World patriotism and anti-bug hysteria sweeping the galaxy in the wake of the invasion has pushed STAR's popularity ratings through the roof once more, and the Authority has reluctantly agreed to increase funding in order to expand the Marine Corps, and end the bug threat once and for all.

Remit & Jurisdiction

You cannot exaggerate about the STAR Marines. They are convinced to the point of arrogance that they are the most ferocious fighters in the galaxy – and even after the discovery of giant, predatory razor-toothed bugs, they're probably right!
– Sir Anthony Falken III, Vice President STAR Industries, 2280

The galaxy is a big place. To date, over 210 planets have been colonized, stretching right across the galactic plane, with countless mining outposts, research bases, hyperspace docks, and space stations spread further still. The location of these systems appears at first to be sporadic – yet they are dictated primarily by their suitability for hyperlane travel, and secondly by their wealth in resources. Those mature systems that have developed to an almost Earth-like level are often referred to as the "core worlds," while those further afield or less well developed are the "fringe colonies." At the epicenter of human expansion are, of course, the Sol system and planet Earth, both the administrative center of the Pan-System Authority and the spiritual home of all humans – even those who have never set foot on "Terran" soil.

Protecting all of this vast territory from potential threats is no easy feat, which is why the STAR Pan-System Marine Corps is organized into such widespread, free-roaming autonomous companies. Though they answer directly to STAR Command – STAR Industries' military control center – the marines have full control over day-to-day tactical decisions and deployments. STAR Command itself is based on Earth's moon, along with the Lunar

General Ibrahim Yeats, Lunar Base Divisional Commander, 2267-71.

Division HQ. The Lunar Regiments are widely regarded as the best of the best, formed one of the largest marine divisions in existence. Though their marines are recruited almost exclusively from the Sol system colonies, SMEUs from the Lunar Division often find themselves dispatched all across the galaxy, making their marines the most well-traveled troopers in the corps.

It is rare for marines to be called upon for domestic actions – this job usually falls to the Terran Army for ground wars against uprisings and territorial disputes, and SolNav for outer space actions and pirate activity – but when elite forces are required on Earth, it is the Lunar Regiments that answer the call. They were the first to the field against the Araknyd incursion, and suffered the brunt of marine casualties during that campaign.

Organization & Standard Operating Procedures

When Captain Ana Carter earned her medal for uncommon valor, I was asked if women have any place in this dirty war we're fighting. Let me tell you this. It doesn't make a jot of difference if a marine is man or woman. They undergo punishing training regimes in a zero-G facility. They kill bugs and follow orders. They inherit the traditions of the marines. They are marines.
– Colonel Abraham T. Stokeley, 5th Arcturian Regiment, STAR Pan-System Marine Corps

STAR Pan-System Marine Corps divisions are usually raised from a singular system, planet, or moon, depending on the military heritage and training facilities available. Most divisions maintain their own divisional HQ – a large military space station or lunar base, for example – which answers directly to STAR Command.

STAR Marine divisions are broken down into a number of regiments, which themselves are divided into autonomous expeditionary units (SMEUs), or companies, each trained to react and adapt to any given combat situation. There can be anywhere between one and ten such companies within a regiment, depending on resources. Members of a SMEU train together, live together, and fight together for their entire careers, creating a close-knit organization. Each company is assigned a sector or range of sub-sectors to patrol, being active and space-borne for the majority of their five-year tour, before returning to a STAR facility for refits, debriefing, and retraining. As a result, unless killed in action or forced to retire, the average STAR Marine will spend more time aboard their Demeter-class cruiser than they will on solid ground. The Demeters are more than just military transports of course – they are mobile barracks, each fitted with training and recreational facilities, large armories, and medical bays. Most are assigned one or more science officers, so that new discoveries made while patrolling the fringe of human territory can be examined, and findings communicated directly to STAR Command.

At full strength, each STAR marine expeditionary unit comprises 72 fighting men and women, plus command, science, medical, and support staff, such as engineering, fleet administration and so on. The SMEU is normally commanded by a colonel, major, or lieutenant-major, who rarely takes the field (although fully trained to do so), but instead operates from within the Demeter as a strategic commander. The remaining members of the SMEU are broken down into three autonomous platoons, each comprising 24 marines and assigned its own medium-range Seraphim dropship. Operationally, a platoon contains four squads – two eight-man fireteams, a four-man field HQ led by a corporal or captain, and a four-man specialist team. The platoon is often called upon to act in isolation, perhaps combating a threat on one world while the other platoons deal with problems elsewhere in a sector – in

(OPPOSITE)
Major Xander of the 9th Tau Ceti Regiment inspects the aftermath of a battle against Araknyds during the Yanto Incursion.

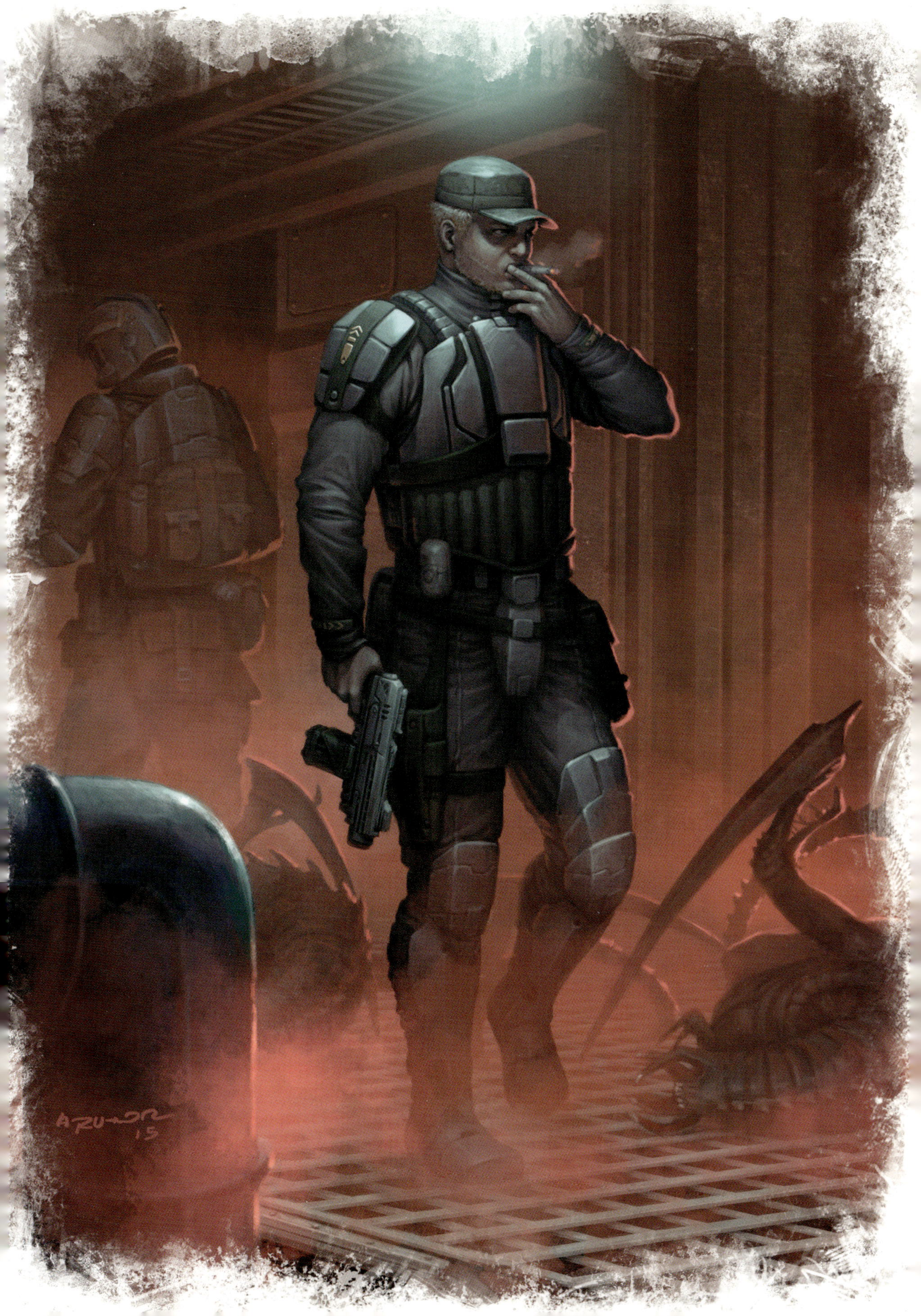

this function the Seraphim dropships take on the role of mobile HQ, and are able to provide resources and supplies for a platoon for up to a month without resupply.

Fireteams

The backbone of the STAR Marine Corps is its fireteams, which make up the majority of the fighting units at the corps' disposal. Each fireteam comprises eight riflemen, including a sergeant. One of these marines is designated a "fire support trooper," and is usually equipped with a specialist weapon, selected specifically for the tactical operation at hand – a combi-carbine, heavy auto-carbine, grenade launcher, flamethrower, or man-portable railgun. One rifleman is always assigned to back up the specialist, acting as spotter, loader, and weapon technician, and taking over the role if the fire support trooper should become incapacitated. The fire support trooper himself always carries a sidearm as backup – usually a frag pistol, "bugstopper," or combat shotgun depending on expertise and aptitude.

The standard armament of the rifleman is the SI-160 assault carbine. These weapons fire enervated caseless ammunition in short controlled bursts, capable of penetrating the toughened hides of most bug strains.

Every member of a fireteam is a highly trained individual, excelling in bug-hunting tactics, and is required to read up on new developments and research whenever there is sufficient downtime. Even without access to the proper chain of command, it is expected that an individual rifleman be able to take responsibility for his own survival, while employing sufficient battle tactics to take the fight to the enemy. The level of trust placed in STAR marines sets them aside from the "grunts" of the Terran Army, SolNav, and the United System Defense (USD) Coastguard, earning them respect and envy in equal measure.

Specialists

In addition to the fireteams, each platoon has a standing force of four specialists, drawn from the SMEU's elite. These marines are sometimes pressed into service as riflemen, having been through the same training and combat maneuvers as the rest of their platoon. However, such deployment is often considered an almost criminal waste of their skills, as these specialists usually undergo several years of supplemental training to fulfill one of several niche battlefield roles.

The most common deployment of a specialist team is as a heavy weapons squad. Whereas one such weapon is usually present in every fireteam, specialists excel at bringing four to bear at once, concentrating their firepower on critical targets, and digging into fortified positions as sappers. Once a heavy weapons squad have become entrenched, they are capable of holding the line with an efficiency that puts most regular fireteams to shame – no mean feat in the elite Marine Corps.

Specialist teams are also trained in the use of the Phalanx combat exo-suit. These powered suits incorporate state-of-the-art armor bonded to a powered exo-skeleton, using technology developed from cybernetic prosthetics and automated assembly line robotics. Each suit effectively transforms a soldier into a one-man army, increasing his strength, speed, and carrying capacity fivefold, and allowing him to wield heavy weaponry with little to no encumbrance. Against larger bug species, the augmented physicality of an exo-suit trooper has often meant the difference between life and death, and the presence of an exo-suit team on the battlefield often engenders great confidence in the other combatants. There are, however, several downsides to the use of exo-suits. Firstly, their numbers are in very short supply, with less than one fully equipped per squad in a SMEU. Secondly, the amount of power required by these suits is astronomical, and a fully charged suit only allows three hours' continuous use, meaning that they are only feasible for rapid strike missions. Finally, as a relatively new innovation, it is as yet unclear what toll prolonged exo-suit use takes on the pilots. As each suit is controlled by means of extensive psi-implants, and hardwired directly into the pilot's neural cortex, it is not unknown for battle-damage to a suit's drive mechanisms to result in trauma to the pilot, just as if he had been wounded himself.

Even rarer than exo-suits, some specialists are now taking to the field with experimental grav-packs, which allow a marine to make an anti-gravity jump and even short periods of sustained flight. When used in coordinated strikes, grav-packs have proven effective in confusing bug "hive minds," presenting a fast-moving target that often leads attacking bugs away from their primary target. Grav-packs are able to lift considerable weight – at least double the weight of the average marine – and are thus ideal for the rapid redeployment of equipment and sentry guns in extreme battlefield conditions.

Surface defence facility, Lunar Regiment HQ.

> **GENERAL IBRAHIM YEATS,
> LUNAR BASE DIVISIONAL COMMANDER, 2267-71**
>
> One of the first marine captains ever to fight against a sentient bug, Ibrahim Yeats fought Xeno-Parasites on Io and Perdition, receiving the corps' highest award for bravery, the purple sun. After being wounded in the Luyten campaign, the then-Colonel Yeats was pulled from active duty, where he rose to the rank of general, eventually taking control of the moon's prestigious marine division. Yeats is notable, however, for his last memorable duty. In 2271 he spoke at a public inquiry on behalf of STAR Command in light of the Marine Corps' previous refusal to engage bugs in the Klaatu Nebula. Deviating radically from his prepared briefing, Yeats spoke passionately about the duty of a marine to protect mankind, and how the incident at Klaatu VI had shamed him to the core. His speech was a deciding factor in the passing of the Pan-System Concordance, which signed additional powers over marine deployment to the Authority. Yeats was hailed a hero at the time by the Authority's ruling council, but died a month later, peacefully in his sleep. He is now all but forgotten.

Some SMEUs are assigned sniper teams amongst their specialists. Given the "horde" nature of most bug threats, sniper teams are rarely seen in interstellar actions. However, there have been occasions when STAR marines have been called in to assist the Terran Army in subjugating human rebellions or internal terrorist threats – in such dire circumstances, the marine snipers are rightly feared for their precision firepower.

Tactics

I don't know if these bugs got religion, and I don't care. I say kill 'em all, and let their stupid bug gods worry about 'em.

– Sergeant Marquez, 12th Lunar Regiment

Cover Formation

The most common environment for STAR marine deployments is confined complexes and tunnel networks, whether performing a surgical strike on a remote colony base, a boarding action against an infested starship or space station, or a nestbusting mission deep within the caverns of an alien hive. The organization of marine platoons into four- and eight-man squads is purely to facilitate standard marine cover formation – the most reliable method of advancing through tight confines, sweeping unexplored territory and taking ground.

Standard sweeping formation requires that two marines take point while two others remain behind to provide covering fire. Once a new position is secure, the point men provide cover while the rearguard move forward, and the process repeats. Eight-man teams follow the same procedure, but simply alternate more frequently – the main advantage of the larger team being that more marines are on hand to sweep rooms or side-tunnels, or hold positions while the remainder continue the sweep.

Surgical Strikes

Against planet-based complexes, marine platoons excel at surgical strikes, operating in a traditional "air cavalry" role. Dropsuit teams hit the site from Seraphim dropships, while the remaining marines usually deploy in Timberwolf APCs which grav-chute in from the air. The priorities of any surgical strike are to (a) secure a field HQ, (b) secure a perimeter and access the combat zone, (c) neutralize hostiles, and (d) rescue survivors. Additional objectives may be prioritized by regimental command on a case-by-case basis.

Draper's World bugs are not to be engaged at close quarters – unless you're equipped with a Phalanx Exo-Suit.

Boarding Actions

STAR marines are trained in anti-grav combat from day one at the academy, and this is primarily so that they can maintain discipline and combat effectiveness while performing boarding actions. When a spacebound ship or facility is infested with bugs, essential systems are usually damaged, leading to a complete loss of artificial gravity and atmosphere. Fireteams, therefore, must often engage the enemy in zero-G conditions, whilst wearing sealed environment armor. Railgun teams invariably lead the way in these operations.

Access to stricken ships is usually provided by eight-man assault boats, which are fired from SMEU cruisers. These boats clamp to any available hatch on the target vessel, and either override the airlock controls or utilize controlled detonations to provide access.

Open War

Often called the worst case scenario or last resort, it is a common marine maxim that warfare against bugs on open ground is an admission of failure. Of course, there have been several successful actions fought in this manner – the first ever campaign against Hive-Beasts on Klaatu VI most notable amongst them. However, the "acceptable" casualty rate during these actions is much higher than normal, given the huge potential for marines to be overrun. On the open battlefield, marines are often forced to fight from defensive positions – a role far more suited to the mass manpower solutions of the Terran Army. Although every marine platoon has access to a small mobile firebase, these are usually used as remote field HQs rather than defensible positions. Where open war is known in advance to be the only logical outcome of a campaign, larger firebases and pre-fab fortifications are dropped from orbit using grav-chutes, and quickly assembled on an advantageous position. From there, marines tend to adopt sniper and long-range tactics, resorting to "firing by ranks" when the enemy waves get closer. This form of warfare had not been used for over 250 years, before the first bugs were discovered – yet it has proven effective once again.

Weapons & Equipment

The following section details the main arms, equipment, and uniform options available to STAR marine fireteams in the field.

SI-160 Assault Carbine

Developed from the much heavier MI-G60 assault rifle used by the Terran Army, the SI-160 is a compact, lightweight, semi-automatic carbine, and has become the standard issue weapon of STAR Marine Corps rifleman fireteams. It is light but incredibly rugged, being constructed from lightweight metal alloys and shock-resistant poly-plastic compounds. The weapon was designed for portability and efficient function in any environment and in any extreme of pressure or temperature. Though it lacks the sheer power of the MI-G60, this is compensated for by the carbine's rate of fire and reliability, and the superior penetration of the enervated 4.73 x 33mm caseless ammunition.

The SI-160 was designed with hordes of fast-moving bugs in mind, fulfilling the need to increase target hit probability by firing high-rate multi-round salvos. Even on the move, the carbine can be fired with remarkable accuracy. Recoil is amongst the lowest for a military-grade weapon of its size category, while jamming and overheating are virtually unheard of. Rounds are fed into the weapon from a magazine that lies below and parallel with the barrel. The rounds are oriented vertically (at 90 degrees to the bore) and are fed upwards into the rotary chamber where they are rotated 90 degrees for firing. This electronic process is powered by an arc-stabilized plasma core and, coupled with a cyclical multi-round breech, results in efficiency unmatched by traditional loading mechanisms. The weapon achieves optimal accuracy in semi-automatic fire mode, firing 3-round bursts. On full-auto mode, the 80-round magazine can be emptied in 4.2 seconds. The ammunition itself contains a charged plasma core, activated via an explosive tip, which causes massive internal damage due to a targeted energy release system without compromising armor penetration.

The SI-160 carbine is fitted as standard with a simple reflector sight. However, for extreme battlefield conditions every marine also carries a snap-fit optical sight with low-power magnification and thermal reticule display.

In addition, every marine carries an underslung grenade launcher, which snaps to the underside of the SI-160's barrel, and carries six 28mm fragmentation grenades, with an effective launch range of 220m. It is unusual in practice for a marine to carry additional grenades, as the reloading procedure is tricky and time-consuming. Accordingly, the grenade launchers are usually prepped and readied before entering the combat zone, even though the fitting of the launcher results in a minor reduction in accuracy.

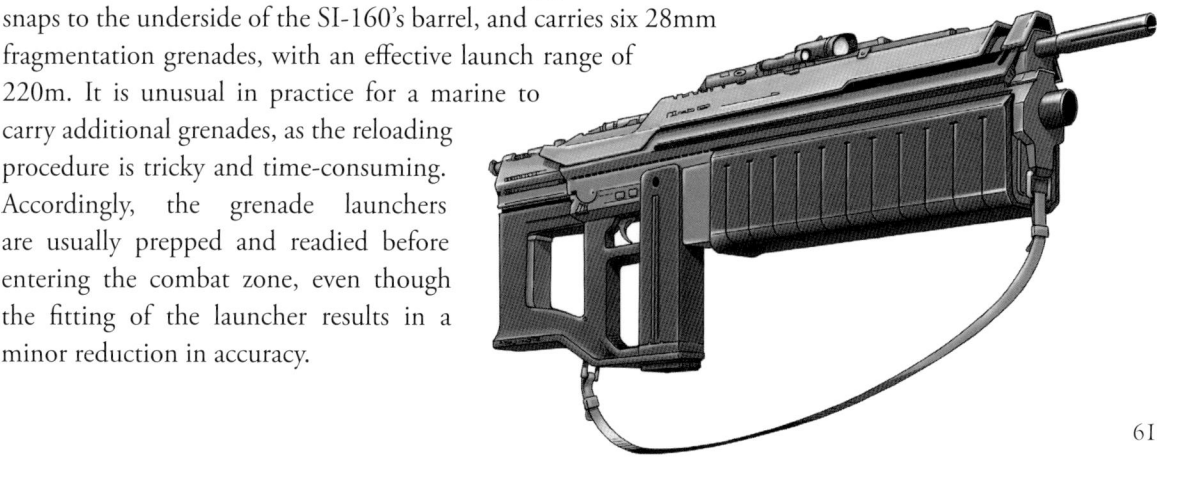

SI-160 Assault Carbine.

SI-200 Combi-carbine

Taking the basic workings of the SI-160, the combi-carbine is a tougher, heavier assault carbine, featuring an underslung secondary weapon housed in a reinforced titanium casing. The standard loadout features a personal flamethrower (see the Model 995 flamethrower, below), with a gel-cartridge good for six bursts. Alternatively, the combi-carbine can be fitted with a pump-action 12-gauge shotgun as a secondary weapon, containing six shells in a hard-fit magazine. Standard scatter ammunition for the shotgun attachment can be replaced with solid slug or anti-chitin capped rounds.

Combi-carbine.

Crossfire Model 32 "Mauler" Frag Pistol

Essentially a semi-automatic pistol shotgun, the Mauler was developed as an effective all-purpose sidearm against chitin-armored bug swarms in close confines. Where a combat shotgun often proves too bulky to form part of a fire support trooper's standard kit, the Model 32 is a good compromise, offering effective stopping power across a "scattergun"-type spread.

Crossfire Model 32 Frag Pistol.

The Mauler's underslung clip contains eight 16-gauge shells, with enervated shot designed for splintering bone and chitin exo-skeletons. Where carrying capacity allows, some marines also carry secondary clips of solid or nitrogen-infused shot; these provide maximum lethality and internal trauma but reduce the area of effect to a single target. Incendiary shot has also been field-tested, but has so far proved ineffective against most types of infestation due to the poor range, accuracy, and burn time.

Crossfire MC12 Combat Shotgun

One of the oldest weapon patterns in the Crossfire arms company's repository, the MC12 has stood the test of time due to its simple design and battlefield effectiveness. A rugged, semi-automatic 12-gauge shotgun, the MC12 is often carried by specialists, fire support troopers, and NCOs as a backup weapon, and is frequently carried aboard APCs for close-quarter assault actions.

The MC12 is a versatile weapon with a variety of ammunition, which can be interchangeably loaded into its 9-shot chamber. It can fire 76 mm shells of differing power levels without any operator adjustments and in any combination. Standard ammo carried on marine operations includes canister (scatter), solid slug, rocket-assisted, high-ex, nitrogen, and anti-chitin capped rounds.

MC12 Combat Shotgun.

SI-66X Heavy Auto-carbine

Dubbed "Frankenstein" by the troops, this heavy-caliber machine gun is an ugly hybrid of the Terran Army's MX250 chaingun and the STAR Marine Corps SI-160 standard-issue carbine. By replacing most of the titanium casing with composite plastics the SI-66X is a much lighter – though still unwieldy – weapon than its groundhog counterpart.

SI-66X Heavy Auto-carbine.

Firing 6.6mm enervated caseless plasma rounds at a rate of 400 rounds per minute, the heavy auto-carbine has to be mounted on a personal harness and suspension system in order to fire with any degree of accuracy. Its ammo hoppers each contain 500 rounds at full capacity. Many fire support troopers use a 900-round belt-feed instead to reduce weight and bulk – however, the removal of the electric drum feed sacrifices rate of fire. The fire support trooper is always assigned a backup marine to carry additional ammunition and assist with maintenance and clearing jams.

The "Frankenstein" is not ideal for bug infestations in close quarters, although standard operating procedure dictates that at least two such weapons are present in any platoon organization. The fire support trooper who carries the SI-66X thus usually carries a secondary firearm for when the sheer size of the Frankenstein is counterproductive.

Model 995 "Snapdragon" Flamethrower

Before mankind encountered dangerous bug strains, the flamethrower had long since been abandoned as a weapon of war, considered too barbaric and inhumane to use on the battlefield. Now, however, it has become a powerful weapon in the war on bugs, especially Araknyds and Hive-Beasts.

Discarding 21st-century thermobaric technology, which is mostly useless in alien atmospheres, the snapdragon instead uses a hydrocarbon gel-pack, which is liquefied and pressurized when the trigger is depressed, and ignited by an external flame as it leaves the barrel. The gel burns with an intense heat, producing its own oxygen to feed the flames as it does so. The burning liquid is incredibly viscous, and sticks to the target, ensuring that it is almost impossible to extinguish the flames until the gel has burned up.

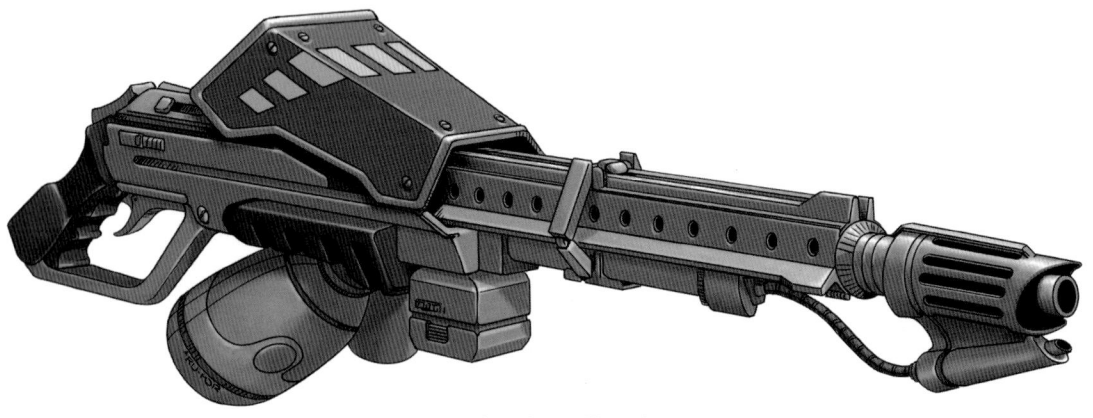

Snapdragon Flamethrower.

Grenades

The Marine Corps utilizes a variety of specialist hand grenades – a highly effective, if often low-tech, solution to 23rd-century battlefield problems.

The standard-issue grenade belt contains two M62 fragmentation grenades and one baffler grenade. The baffler grenade releases a cloud of dense smoke, thermal particles, and an electromagnetic scrambler screen, essentially making visual and scan-assisted targeting impossible. Against some species of bug – especially Araknyds – the electromagnetic screen seems to interfere with synaptic relays as well as messing up their vision, temporarily confusing the beasts.

Any of the grenades may be replaced with anti-chitin or nitrogen grenades at the behest of a platoon's commanding officer. Developed from anti-armor charges, anti-chitin grenades work much like an old-fashioned "nail bomb," discharging a cloud of armor-piercing high-explosive shells into the midst of an enemy formation. These shells can penetrate or embed themselves in chitinous armor up to 2 inches thick, whereupon they explode with some force, ripping chunks out of bug hides. Nitrogen grenades, on the other hand, release an expanding core of enervated liquid nitrogen, instantly freezing anything they touch. These are tailored for combat against the Draper's World Xeno-Parasite – although it cannot kill them outright, it does make them extremely sluggish for vital seconds or even minutes.

Thermal detonators are not standard issue, and are usually carried in addition to the regulation grenade pack. They are based on the Terran Army's incendiary grenades, but are larger to accommodate a greater amount of thermate and an increased charge for wider dispersion. These grenades spread a flaming chemical compound around the detonation point, burning in excess of 3,992°F (2,200°C), in almost any atmosphere as no external oxygen source is required. After seeing the effectiveness of incendiary grenades against Araknyds during the Earth invasion, these larger packs were developed hastily for marine patrols taking the fight to the enemy.

"Nestbuster" Smart Nuke

Despite its name, the smart nuke is not a nuclear weapon in the old-fashioned sense, in that it does not require fission-fusion or fissile materials such as plutonium or uranium. Instead, the smart nuke uses a low-yield pure fusion core, which explodes with incredible power, but creates no nuclear fallout.

The smart nuke was originally developed to combat Araknyd nests, but has also proven invaluable against Hive-Beast colonies. It is a man-portable device, resembling a heavy sphere some 9 inches in diameter. Once activated, the sphere separates, and its central gravitic drive propels it upwards to a height of around 6 1/2 feet. The on-board guidance system follows trace chemical signatures emitted by the bugs, gliding through subterranean tunnels, maintenance shafts, and corridors, eventually detonating when the

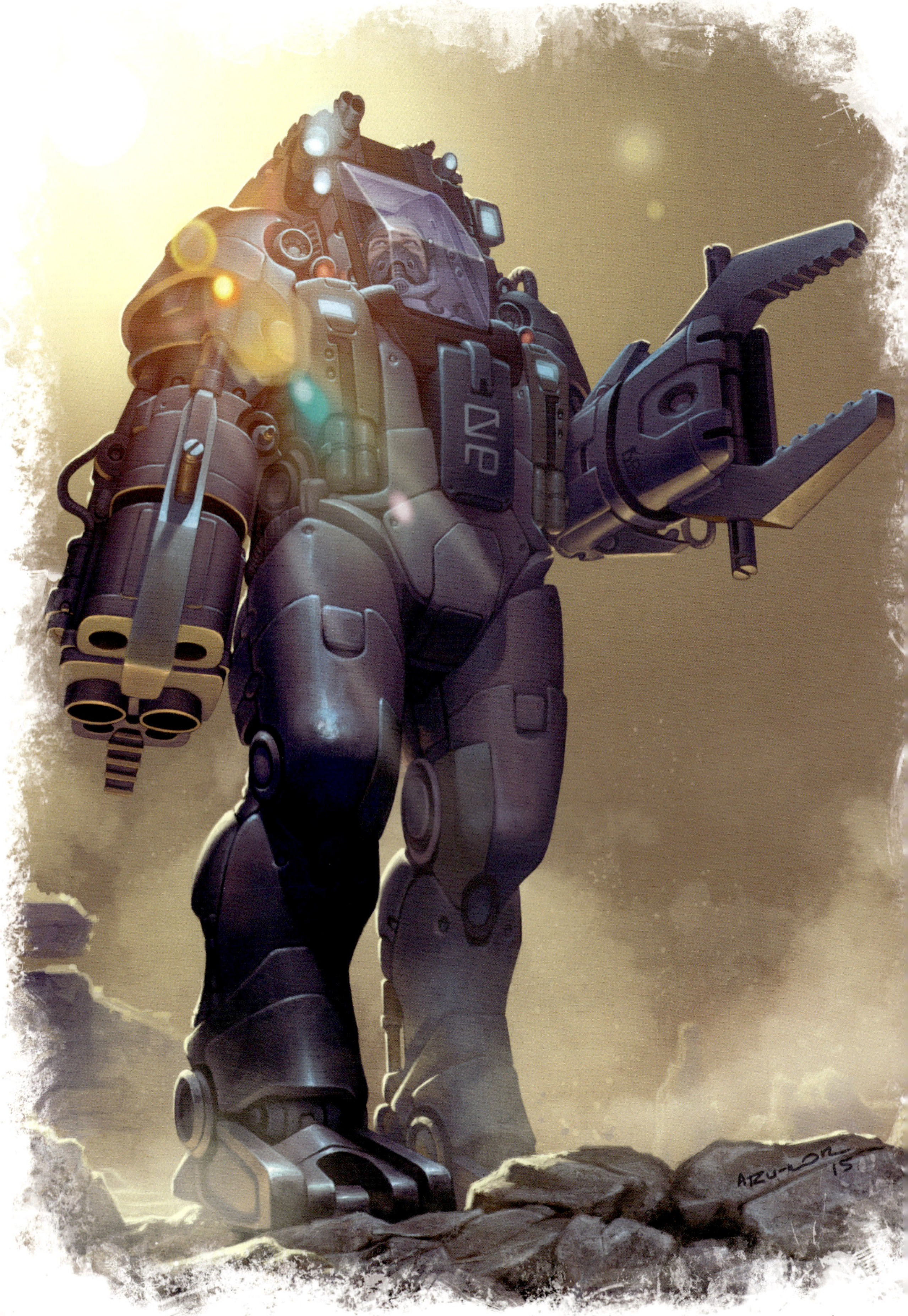

concentration of those signatures reaches a critical point – this is usually an indicator that a bug nest has been discovered.

The power of the smart nuke is usually enough to eradicate all but the largest nests, and recent trials using the on-board sensors to detect hive-beast and Xeno-Parasite trace signatures have proven moderately successful. However, the weapon is bulky before it is activated, has a limited range (of around 550 yards), and is incredibly expensive to manufacture. Marine doctrine forbids the use of smart nukes unless thorough battlefield surveys have first been conducted. Pre-emptive use – and therefore wastage – of these valuable weapons is punishable by court martial.

TGL-40 Lockdown, 40mm Tactical Grenade Launcher

The TGL-40 is a robust multi-shot grenade launcher, featuring a semi-automatic launcher fed by a 9-shot rotary magazine. The TGL-40 is a bulky weapon, weighing over 60 pounds unloaded, and is therefore usually mounted on a suspension harness in much the same way as a heavy auto-carbine. The TGL-40 can also be tripod-mounted or emplaced on the cupola mount of a Timberwolf APC. It fires specially designed 40x50mm frag, incendiary, or anti-chitin cartridges. Occasionally, spare hoppers of baffler grenades are carried by the fire support troopers, but against many bug species these often prove ineffective.

The TGL-40 also contains an on-board X5 smart processor, a computerized targeting system that automatically calculates the angle of fire to attack enemies behind cover, priming frag grenades so that they detonate in an airburst above emplaced positions. This fire mode can also be combined with anti-chitin grenades, utilizing a short-ranged homing system to "pursue" bugs into warrens and tunnels before detonating.

(OPPOSITE)
Marine specialist of the 6th Magellan Regiment in Phalanx Combat Exo-suit.

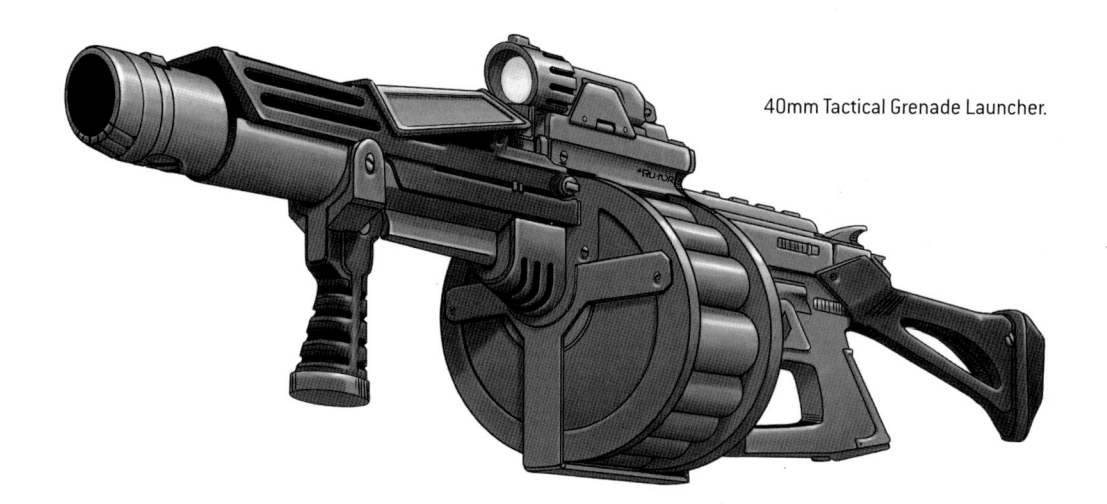

40mm Tactical Grenade Launcher.

Firestorm Launcher Harness

A bulky weapon usually confined to use by exo-suit specialists, the Firestorm is a personal grenade launcher harness, which mounts six 28mm frag grenades upon a chest-mounted strap. The delivery system is activated by pulling the safety cord and slapping a trigger mechanism on the marine's shoulder. After a five-second delay, the launcher then fires its full payload, one at a time, creating a storm of shrapnel from which the harness derives its name. Exo-suits usually mount two of these harnesses, controlled via the suit's neuro-link.

KT-EM4 Man-portable Railgun

Created by cutting-edge arms manufacturer KarmaTek, the KT-EM4 is one of the most valued long-range weapons in the STAR Marine Corps' arsenal. Utilizing the same electromagnetic rail technology as starship-mounted rail cannons, which were developed to eliminate recoil completely, man-portable railguns have no kick whatsoever, yet enjoy superior range and penetration over conventional firearms. The EM4's barrel comprises a pair of parallel conducting rails, along which a sliding armature is accelerated by the electromagnetic effects of a current that flows down one rail, into the armature and then back along the other rail. By charging the weapon with a phased plasma core carried on the marine's back, the weapon can accelerate a solid slug to hypersonic velocities of approximately 1 1/2 miles per second, or about Mach 7. This kinetic energy provides unparalleled armor penetration even at extreme range, and railgun rounds have been known to penetrate up to 2 feet of concrete, and even herculanium plating.

Mk IV Combat Blade

This reinforced, high-tensile carbon-polymer blade is issued to every STAR marine upon graduation from the academy, along with his uniform and carbine. It is a single-handed heavy fighting knife, with a blade length of 9 1/2 inches (nearly an inch longer than the Terran Army equivalent), a single serrated edge and a razor-sharp monofilament slicing edge. The Mk IV also utilizes a bayonet conversion clip in the hilt, allowing it to be snapped to the SI-160 carbine in place of the underslung grenade launcher.

The Mk IV is such an intrinsic part of marine mentality that it is treasured more than the carbine. Although it is specially designed to withstand the extremes of temperature and bio-acid contamination that are a hazard of fighting some alien races, against bugs of any strain its use is considered desperate or even foolhardy – the maxim goes that "if you're close enough to stick a knife in the thing, you're already dead." However, the Mk IV is a survival tool as well as a combat weapon – though that doesn't stop marines from training in knife-fighting techniques, and even sleeping with their knife in easy reach.

Mk IV Combat Blade.

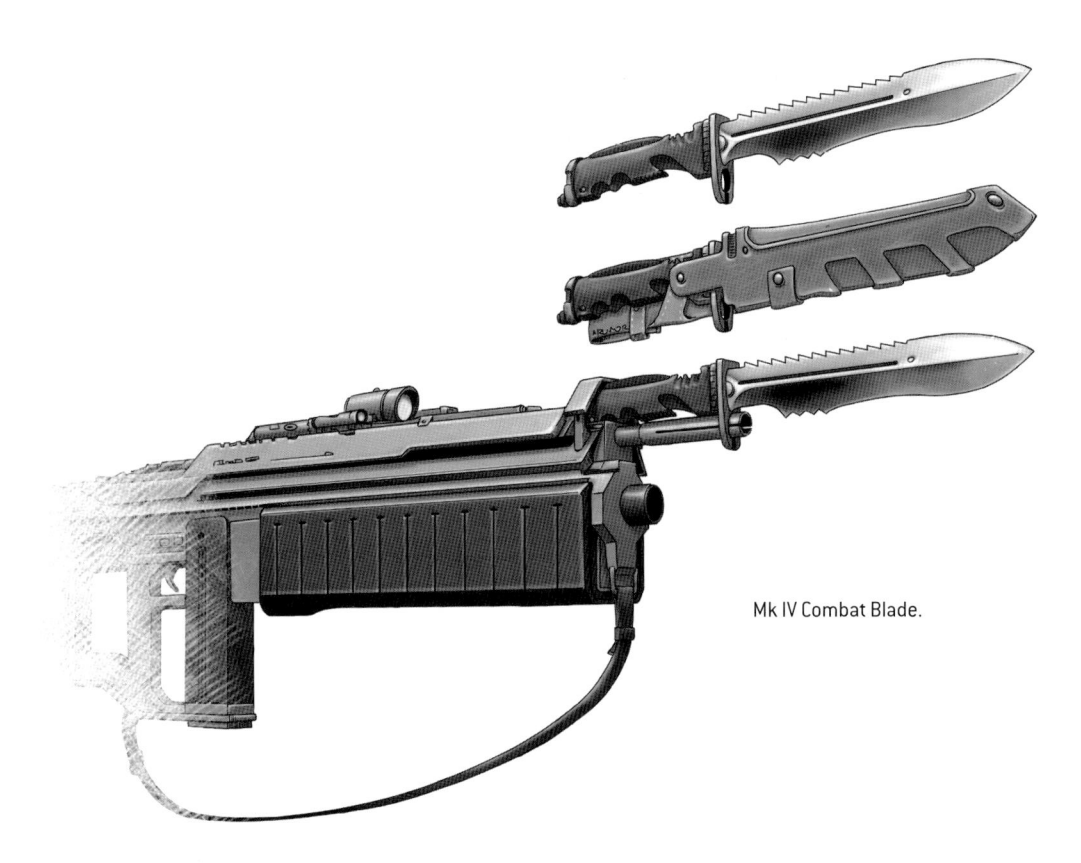

SIS-45 "Bugstopper" Tactical Sidearm

Issued primarily to Seraphim and Timberwolf crews, NCOs, and senior officers, and supplied as standard stowage aboard Phalanx exo-suits, the SIS-45 is a powerful .45 cal semi-automatic pistol. Very much viewed as an emergency or "backup" weapon, the sidearm is light yet robust, and although poor at penetrating thick chitin exo-armor, it is a precision weapon, easily capable of bringing down smaller bugs. Any marine carrying a Bugstopper is issued two 7-shot magazines of anti-chitin explosive rounds, to complement the standard-issue hollow-points. The weapon also features a number of optional snap-fit components, such as weapon light, night-vision scope, and shoulder stock, though the latter two are rarely carried in the field.

SIS-45 Tactical Sidearm.

PBX500 Longrifle

Although long-ranged firepower in the modern Marine Corps is often the domain of the railgun, there are still occasions when sniper teams are required to hold positions or provide accurate fire support from long range. The railgun is notoriously sensitive, and at extreme range can prove inaccurate. Enter the PBX500 – the perfect sniper's weapon.

SI-242 Emplaced Rotary Cannon

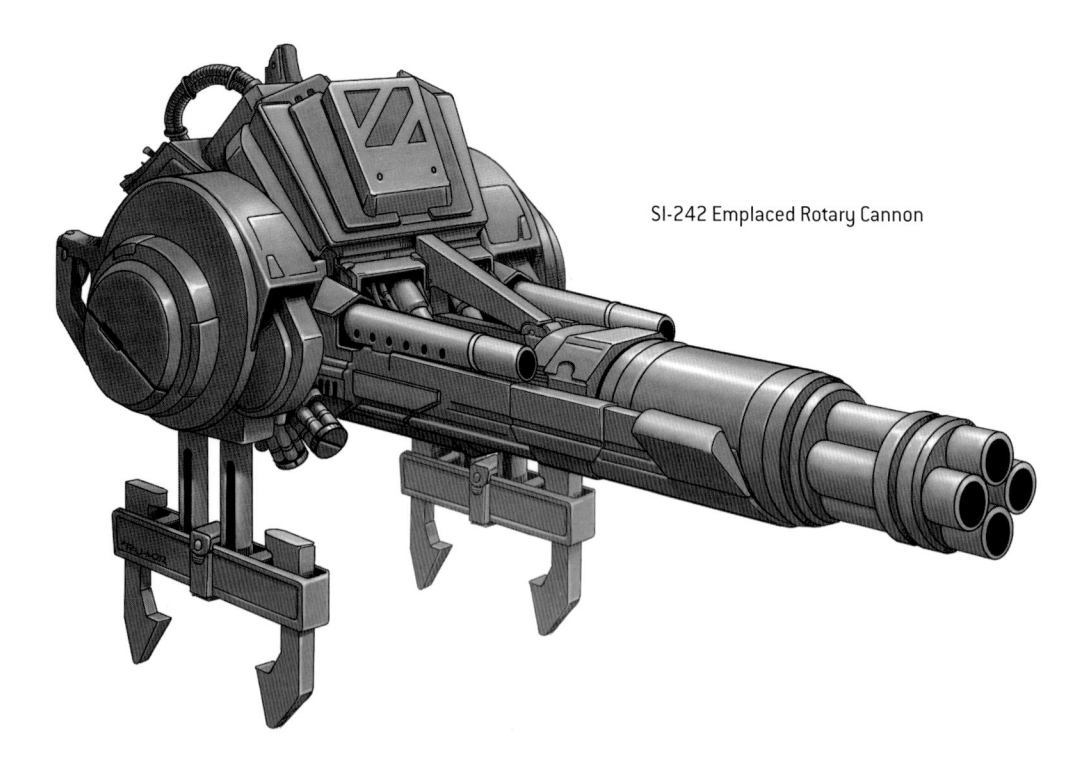

The .50 cal semi-automatic longrifle is equipped with armor-piercing rounds, stabilizer clamps, and computer-assisted smart targeting system, featuring night-vision sights and manual override. The barrel is muffled for stealth operations. Standard ammunition is effective at ranges of up to 1,100 yards. Nitrogen-core rounds are available for actions against Xeno-Parasites, while the arms manufacturer Purdey-Browning has recently unveiled its heat-seeking, thermal detonation, and computer-guided rounds, which have already begun testing in regimental training facilities.

SI-242 "Devastator" Emplaced Rotary Cannon

Firing 12mm enervated caseless plasma rounds through four motorized rotating barrels at a rate of 1,000 rounds per minute, the Devastator is one of the most fearsome guns in the STAR marine arsenal. Almost impossible to wield in a man-portable capacity due to its bulk (though many have tried), the Devastator is most often fitted to vehicle couplings, or affixed to temporary fortifications by means of its auto-clamp and smart rail system.

When firing continuously, the titanium motor has a lifespan of around 600,000 rounds, and the barrels are prone to overheating, visibly glowing red as the super-charged ammo is fed through them.

Aegis XT Automated Sentry Gun

The Aegis XT is an automated turret-based weapon platform that uses thermal imaging to lock onto human-sized targets at up to 1,400 yards. Utilizing motion tracking and infra-red targeting systems, the computerized target matrix is most effective when multiple guns are set up at strategic choke-points, triangulating targets and laying down a devastating web of suppression fire.

The basic Aegis rig is man-portable, and is easily set up on a fixed tripod by a single fireteam. Some success has been had with remote-controlled tracked Aegis units, though their testing has so far been limited.

The Aegis XT rig can mount either a single SI-242 Rotary Cannon, twin heavy auto-carbines, or tri-linked SI-160s, fed via a large ammo drum at the rear of the unit.

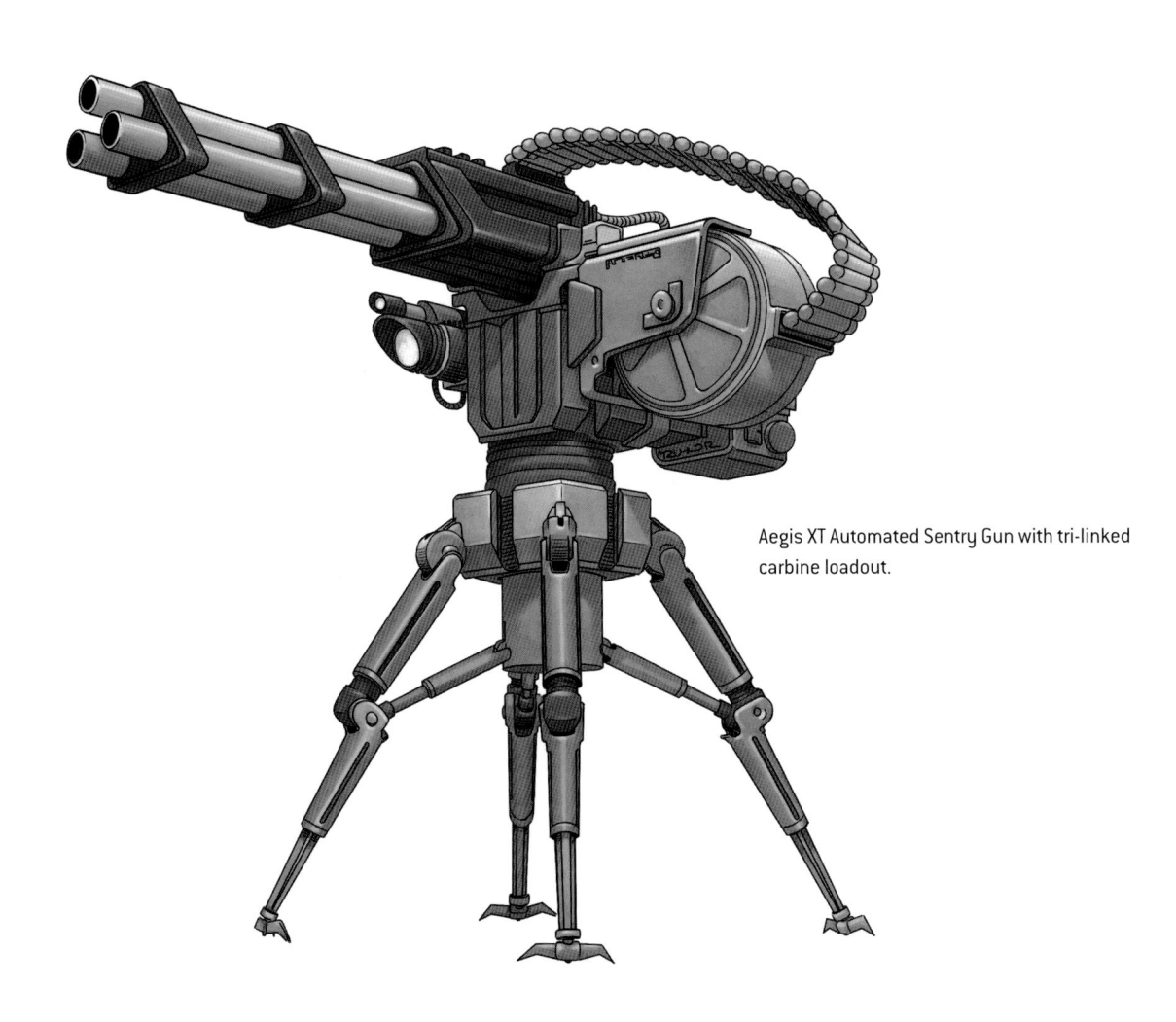

Aegis XT Automated Sentry Gun with tri-linked carbine loadout.

STAR Interceptor Combat Armor

Combining a suit of tough dura-weave fatigues with an armored tactical vest and titanium boot-guards, the standard-issue combat armor is designed to protect marines from small arms fire, stab wounds, slashing claws, and acidic residue. When fighting in extreme temperatures, or notably against Draper's World Xeno-Parasites, marines are often issued with a heat-resistant Kevlar-weave fatigue instead of the standard Interceptor suit. Though it has often been mooted that advanced armors are the future in the war against bugs, light infantry combat armor such as STAR's Interceptor pattern provides a low-cost mass-produced solution to 30 percent of potentially incapacitating injuries sustained at range, without compromising mobility or efficiency. The armor incorporates a twin ammo/grenade harness with universal suspension adapter fittings for heavy weapons, a utility belt, boot-mounted knife-sheath, and snap-fit backpack.

STAR marine fatigues are normally gray in color, although the dura-weave contains low-spectrum reactive threads that tint the uniform to match battlefield conditions. In addition, spare suits of "adaptive camo" fatigues are usually carried about the SMEU cruiser. Of all bug types encountered, only 25 percent markedly rely on visual acuity when hunting their prey – notably the Centauran Araknyds – and against these aliens, camouflage is a simple but effective tactic.

Mk II Tactical Helmet

Featuring lightweight titanium and duratanium plates, the Mk II tactical helmet offers effective battlefield protection as well as incorporating many tactical features. The helmet includes a long-range midi-comm unit as standard, a flip-down photo-reactive visor with integrated targeting and status head-up display (HUD), and a side-mounted power-beam torch. A port is fitted beneath the torch to include an optional helmet-cam, broadcasting infra-red images along with the marine's vital signs and ammo levels directly back to field HQ.

Phalanx Combat Exo-suit

Considered by many to be the greatest innovation in the marine arsenal, the Phalanx exo-suit is a large suit of powered armor, which transforms the incumbent specialist into a walking tank. By means of a system of tiny electrodes and neuro-links, the seemingly cumbersome armored suit becomes like a second skin to the marine, mimicking his movements and responding to his thoughts instantaneously.

The basic frame of the suits is a servo-assisted exo-skeleton, standing around 8 1/2 feet tall, which vastly increases the strength of the pilot. Herculanium armor plates are bolted to this frame, while the pilot himself is enclosed within a hazard suit and pressurized tactical helmet, featuring advanced

THE FUTURE OF THE STAR MARINES – EXPERIMENTAL TECH AND DARK SCIENCE

Ever since sentient bugs were first discovered, scientists and engineers at STAR Industries have worked tirelessly to create new weapons to aid in the destruction of the alien menace. Some of these innovations, such as smart nukes, dropsuits, thermal detonators, and man-portable railguns, have already found their way into marine regiments. Bug pheromone spray, developed from the carcasses of slain Hive-Beasts, has also proved effective. Other experimental hardware has yet to be field-tested, and is developed in secret facilities away from the prying eyes of the media. The galaxy is not yet ready to learn exactly what STAR Industries has been working on for all these years, although the Araknyd invasion of Earth has certainly whetted public appetite for victory at any cost.

STAR Industries has already experimented with so-called "Trojan Bugs" – remote controlled bugs, potentially carrying explosives, used to infiltrate bug nests. Against beasts with synaptic control mechanisms, these have been unsuccessful, although scientists have not given up hope of perfecting the technology. Another fringe science division has begun to reverse engineer alien weaponry, developing semi-organic energy weapons capable of generating Araknyd plasma. Most disturbing of all, however, is the clone testing. Pushing at the boundaries of so-called "dark science," it is whispered that in secret facilities clone troopers are being grown in vats, mixing human and bug DNA. Some of the less ethically minded scientists at STAR Industries envision a time when no true human is put in danger on the battlefield, but instead stronger, faster soldiers are tailored for each warzone. Soldiers with the ingenuity of humans, but the boiling blood and chitinous bones of Xeno-Parasites, the psychic abilities of Hive-Beasts, or the razor-sharp talons and bio-energy weaponry of Araknyds…

HUD and targeting systems. Powered by an integral miniaturized fusion core, its range is low, but the suits can be recharged using simple plug-in ports present in all marine APCs and Demeter-class cruisers. At full capacity, the suit enables the marine to lift in excess of 1,500 pounds, and sprint at speeds of around 28 miles per hour. The suits are armed with servo-pincers as standard, modified from factory auto-loader units, and usually mounted with arc-cutters and buzz-saws for heavy duty field repair work. The universal snap-fit system adopted by most marines' kit also extends to the exo-suit – shoulder and forearm mounts allow for the positioning of railguns, combi-carbines, heavy auto-carbines, and flamethrowers. Up to two such weapons can be snapped to the suit's hard-points due to the limitations of the HUD controls. Furthermore, most specialists fit grenade harnesses to the suit's torso as a defensive countermeasure.

In addition to their power draining, the suits have proven unreliable in extremes of temperature, with sub-zero cold in particular causing their servos to seize up. In combat zones, this has made them a particularly poor choice against Araknyd swarms, which thrive in arctic conditions.

ARK35 "Archangel" Dropsuit

Developed for rapid insertion tactics, the Archangel dropsuit is a lightweight, armored extension of the standard combat armor, featuring a grav-pack, shock-absorbing boots, and re-breather apparatus. The grav-pack is a personal jet pack consisting of an anti-gravitic booster and leg-mounted stabilizer thrusters. One of the newest innovations in the STAR arsenal, it was initially developed to slow the decent of a freefalling marine, much like an old-fashioned parachute, but has recently been employed for its jump functionality, making rapid redeployment of specialists much easier than in the past. Extensive field testing amongst elite specialist units has proven promising, and the STAR Marine Corps hopes that the packs will be rolled out to all marines as standard kit within the next decade.

Like exo-suits, grav-packs require considerable energy in order to function. However, unlike exo-suits, this energy is only required in very short bursts, and is thus generated in combat via means of a phased plasma-cell, which automatically charges between jumps. Ten minutes of charge produces enough power for three minutes of controlled flight, several short "hops" of around 30 yards, or five minutes of anti-grav gliding.

Spartan Armored Environment Suit

The Spartan suit combines the protection of Interceptor armor with the sealed environment of a spacesuit and sterile hazmat functionality. Designed to allow marines to fight in any atmosphere, or even deep space, the suit is bulky and requires extensive training if it is to be used effectively. The pressurized sections of the suit are compartmentalized, so that tears or damage sustained in battle are unlikely to compromise the entire suit. The marine's torso, shoulders, and chest are protected by thick armor plates, which also cover a small oxygen reservoir, air filtration unit, combat drug injector, and heart-rate regulator.

ART-4 Multi-tracker

A handheld scanner, usually carried by either a squad sergeant or fire support marine, the ART-4 combines computerized cartography, smart blueprint reader, motion-tracker, heat sensors, and biological scanner, all housed in a tough rubberized herculanium casing. It can detect incoming life-signs at a distance of around 900 yards, and movement of anything larger than a household cat at around 550 yards. Using sophisticated positioning tech, the tracker's readout can provide marines with a 3D tactical map of their combat zone, complete with enemy locations.

ART-4 Multi-tracker.

Netrunner Remote Sensor Unit

Carried within the stowage of most Timberwolf APCs, the Netrunner RSU is an unmanned tracked vehicle, remotely controlled from a station in the APC's cockpit. Developed from the Terran Army's bomb disposal robots, the Netrunner carries a larger and more sophisticated multi-tracker system, with long-range scanners and comms arrays. When stationed at strategic battlefield points, the Netrunner can boost ground comms to orbiting command cruisers, and forewarn fireteams of long-distance enemy movements.

Some expeditionary units carry remote breacher kits in addition to sensor units. These kits simply mount twin 40mm grenade launchers on the standard tracked unit, along with a smart nuke that can be remotely primed. The unit also carries a bug pheromone dispersal system to mask its movements. So far, remote "nestbusting" operations have proven unsuccessful due to poor comms within the belly of the larger hives and nest systems, but work continues on developing these tracked exterminators, and AI processors will potentially be added to them to allow independent operation.

Vehicles & Spacecraft

SIMC Epsilon-class Hyperlane Station

Length: 10,500 feet
Beam: 7,875 feet
Draught: 1,680 feet
Crew: 1,280 (permanent); up to 750 (temporary)
Engines: STAR Industries gravitic impulse drive (emergency handling only)
Range: Unlimited (plasma core life 42 years)
Armament: Advanced STAR class 2 defense grid

Positioned at strategic hyperlane jump-gates, these marine facilities provide temporary stations for SMEUs in need of rearmament, ship refits, or just R&R. Providing docking facilities for up to six Demeter-class cruisers, and bristling with defensive weaponry, 18 of these space stations provide an all-too-thin line of STAR control across a massive galaxy.

SIMC Demeter-class Long-range Tactical Cruiser

Length: 3,203 feet
Beam: 760 feet
Draught: 501 feet
Crew: 125
Engines: 3 Rolls Royce Mk VII fusion engines; STAR Industries interstellar plasma drive
Range: Unlimited (plasma core life 15 years)
Armament: 2 turret-mounted KT EM-5000 rail-cannon, fore and aft; 4 railgun broadside banks; 2 fore plasma torpedo tubes; 3 X10 thermonuclear void-to-surface bombs

Designed by Cygnus AeroTech, the Demeter-class cruiser has become the most important innovation in the highly competitive field of interstellar transport vessels. The Demeter is a large military transport, capable of FTL travel and featuring every facility a SMEU requires to complete its tour without ever returning to base.

The Demeter boasts a similar armament to the heavier Kennedy-class warships that protect the core worlds, but is designed first and foremost as a mobile command center, training facility, and barracks for a full STAR Marine Corps expeditionary unit and associated support. Unlike the Kennedy-class warships, the Demeter utilizes advanced gravity field generators by means of a rotating mid-section – as STAR marines are expected to live aboard the cruiser for anything up to five years, a zero-G environment would compromise the physical strength of the marines and place undue stress on their psyche. The training facilities on board the Demeter do include zero-G training chambers, but the artificial gravity systems also allow for pressurized dive pools and

MSS *Bodega*, Lincoln-class Corvette.

environmental simulators, not to mention some perks of the role, such as fresh food from the hydroponics labs and various R&R facilities.

In its vast hold, the Demeter carries three Seraphim dropships, each capable of carrying a marine platoon and two APCs into battle. Most Demeter-class cruisers also carry a handful of endo/exo-atmospheric fighters and their specially trained marine aerospace crews – ever since the discovery of the Araknyd asteroids, they have been a common addition to the Demeters' complements to intercept potentially sentient deep-space bug transports.

Though Demeter-class cruisers have rarely been forced to use their emergency evacuation procedures, all of them carry a full complement of eight-man lifeboats, each containing automated "return-to-base" navicom AI, and cryo-pods to protect the evacuees during their long voyage home.

SN Lincoln-class Corvette

Length: 1,129 feet
Beam: 363 feet
Draught: 402 feet
Crew: 42
Engines: 2 Rolls Royce Mk III fusion engines; STAR Industries phased core hyperdrive
Range: 400 light years (jump); 4 months (fusion propulsion).
Armament: Prow-mounted KT EM-900 rail-cannon; 2 railgun broadside banks; turret-mounted railgun battery; 10 turret-mounted K12 ALRVM anti-fighter missiles

Originally designed for use by SolNav, the Lincoln-class corvette is a medium-range interstellar fighting vessel, featuring a heavy offensive payload for its size and a moderate transport capacity. Twelve of these vessels were purchased for use in the STAR Pan-System Marine Corps in 2242, and heavily modified to allow for the transportation and fast launch of a single marine platoon mounted in a Seraphim dropship. After seeing heavy action in the last two decades, only five of these aging craft remain.

The Lincolns remain one of the fastest fighting vessels in military service, although their design and size does not allow for easy upgrading of their propulsion units. Additionally, only the command bridge retains artificial gravity functionality thanks to an antiquated spinning mid-section. Consequently, these corvettes are generally deemed unsuitable for long tours, but are often found accompanying Demeter-class cruisers as part of small combat fleets, or serving as escorts for civilian vessels in regions where a small marine presence is deemed a necessity.